MURDER IN THE PAINTED MASK

A 1920S COZY HISTORICAL MYSTERY

A GINGER GOLD MYSTERY
BOOK TWENTY-SEVEN

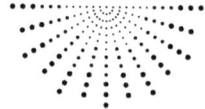

LEE STRAUSS

Library and Archives Canada Cataloguing in Publication

Title: Murder in the Painted Mask / Lee Strauss.

Names: Strauss, Lee (Novelist), author.

Series: Strauss, Lee (Novelist). Ginger Gold mystery ; 27.

Description: Series statement: A Ginger Gold mystery ; book 27 | "A 1920s cozy historical mystery."

Identifiers: Canadiana (print) 20250271559 | Canadiana (ebook) 20250271567 | ISBN 9781774095683

(softcover) | ISBN 9781774095676 (EPUB) | ISBN 9781774095690 (Kindle) | ISBN 9781774095706 (PDF)

Subjects: LCGFT: Cozy mysteries. | LCGFT: Novels.

Classification: LCC PS8637.T739 M8795 2025 | DDC C813/.6—dc23

CHAPTER ONE

The dining room at Hartigan House glowed beneath the soft electric lights of the chandelier, a warm haven against the late December chill that crept through South Kensington. Outside, a fine mist clung stubbornly to the windows, blurring the glow of the street lamps. Inside, however, the air was rich with the aroma of Mrs. Beasley's roasted pheasant, rosemary potatoes, and the hint of cloves wafting from the parsnip soup. The snowy table linen gleamed between fine bone China and polished silver. Decorations of holly, crimson ribbons, and scented candles graced the sideboard and mantel.

Ginger Gold glanced around the table, allowing herself a quiet smile. These dinners, in their own way, were her anchor—a cherished moment to gather her family before the unpredictable demands of society, business, or less savoury pursuits intervened. Or in this case, more holiday festivities that lay ahead.

Her husband Basil, seated across from her at the head of the table, carved the pheasant with the precision of a surgeon. Ginger loved watching him—the way the lines around his hazel eyes deepened when he concentrated, more pronounced now than when they'd first met. The grey streak at his temples, broader than before, only made him look more distinguished.

She turned her attention to the meal. "I must say, Mrs. Beasley has outdone herself once again," she said.

A cheer of agreement rose from those present: Felicia, Ginger's sister-in-law from her first marriage; her husband Charles, Lord Davenport-Witt, the Earl of Witt; Felicia's grandmother Ambrosia, the dowager Lady Gold; and Basil and Ginger's adopted son Scout. Their two-year-old daughter Rosa was already snug in her bed in the nursery, being competently watched over by Nanny Green.

"Hear, hear," Charles said, raising his glass. His

dark hair was neatly parted, his evening jacket impeccably tailored, a picture of aristocratic ease. "And the claret—a perfect vintage, that."

"It's so lovely having everyone here," Ginger said warmly, her gaze settling on Scout, home from boarding school for the holidays. At fourteen, he was navigating that peculiar stretch between boy and man—a hint of fuzzy stubble along his jaw, limbs awkwardly too long for his shirts and trousers. His sandy brown hair flopped slightly over one eye.

"It's good to be home, Mum," Scout replied, his ears reddening slightly. He sat up straighter and flashed a mischievous grin. "Though the holidays always feel far too short. Perhaps I'll stay a bit longer."

"If you do, I suspect Miss Braddock will come here and drag you back herself," Felicia quipped, eliciting a round of gentle laughter.

"With her infamous ruler in hand," Scout added, grinning.

Ginger laughed along, smoothing the bodice of her evening gown of pale green silk. A strand of pearls rested at her collarbone, and her bobbed red hair was styled in soft finger waves, pinned with sequinned clips at her temples. Scout attended a school specialising in equine studies, and Ginger knew he thrived there. In truth, if it weren't for the two horses on the Hartigan House property—Goldmine and Sir Blackwell—he might not return home so willingly.

Under the table, Boss, Ginger's Boston terrier, patrolled with professional intent, his black-and-white nose twitching eagerly at every enticing aroma. Out of the corner of her eye Ginger saw that Lizzie, the maidservant, standing beside Mrs. Beasley the housekeeper as they served, stifled a smile at the dog's optimism. Settling by Ginger's ankles, Boss was rewarded with a discreet sliver of roasted pheasant.

Ambrosia, seated regally at the opposite end of the table, surveyed them all with her usual commanding stare. Her gown of deep violet satin shimmered beneath the chandelier, and her coiffed silver hair was pinned beneath a comb set with amethysts. As she lifted her glass with careful precision, her aged hand, its thin skin revealing dark veins, quivered slightly beneath the weight of the heavy baubles she insisted upon wearing.

"Let us be thankful for a year nearly behind us, and for the promise of the one about to arrive," she intoned.

"To 1929," Ginger said, raising her glass.

The rest echoed, "To 1929."

As the meal continued, the conversation meandered along familiar and foreign shores.

"The talkies have certainly taken London by storm," Felicia said, as she pushed her hair behind one ear. "*The Jazz Singer* seems to have opened a floodgate."

"I heard the Prince of Wales attended a screening last week," Ginger added.

"Better the cinema than the headlines," Charles remarked. "Baldwin back in office again—for now."

"And Ramsay MacDonald waits in the wings," Ambrosia said, dabbing her lips with her napkin. "Politics have become a revolving door, it seems."

"The Americans never fail to dazzle," Basil continued. "Lindbergh across the Atlantic, and now this 'dance craze' is sweeping Mayfair."

"And Wall Street climbing ever higher," Ginger added thoughtfully. "It all feels rather... breathless."

"Frothy is the word, love," Basil said, adjusting his cufflinks.

Outside, the wind whistled faintly around the eaves. A branch scraped against the windowpane, drawing Scout's attention.

"Sounds like rain again," he said.

"Yes," Ginger murmured, her gaze drifting

toward the darkened window. "We've a long drive to the Chilterns at the end of the week. I do hope it lifts by then."

"That you are going is utter madness," Ambrosia declared. "You will drive fifty miles to attend a party at some eccentric artist's invitation? And in Buckinghamshire of all places. The roads will be impassable."

"We've already accepted the invitation, Grandmother," Ginger replied gently. "We can hardly draw back now."

"Especially since Lucien Valentino wouldn't take kindly to being snubbed," Charles added. "He's the sort to remember such things—and retaliate in paint."

"Besides," Basil said, "if we don't go, the rumours would start flying anyway. Best to show our faces, endure the pageantry, and retreat with our reputations intact."

"You make it sound like a military operation," Felicia said with a faint smile.

Basil raised a brow. "In some ways, it is."

Lizzie entered with dessert: a glossy treacle tart crowned with clotted cream. Plates passed around.

"Lucien Valentino's parties are always extravagant," Ginger continued lightly, sensing the shift in tone. "I believe we have Charles to thank for the invitation."

"Ah yes," Charles said, arching an eyebrow. "I met him years ago in connection with the Royal Academy. Valentino was—is—a prodigious talent. And an unrivalled provocateur. Our paths crossed recently, and he insisted Felicia and I attend this shindig. Of course, *I* insisted that all of you join my party."

"The Valentino person's reputation precedes him," Ambrosia said primly. "Noblemen painted as satyrs? Duchesses as Greek goddesses? It's quite... unorthodox."

"Unorthodox is polite," Charles replied with a knowing chuckle. "Scandalous is closer to the mark."

"All the more reason I'm surprised Felicia has still not decided what she's wearing," Ginger said with a teasing smile.

Felicia hesitated. Her dark hair was styled in a sleek, chin-length bob that framed her teardrop-shaped face with elegant precision. The cut was modern, daring even, and perfectly suited her taste for understated glamour. Tonight, she wore a midnight blue dress with subtle beading at the cuffs and neckline—chic yet restrained. Her eyes dropped briefly to her dessert.

"Felicia?" Ginger pressed gently. Felicia adored parties; her lack of enthusiasm was unusual.

"Valentino's gatherings attract a certain... element," Felicia said carefully. "Not everyone invited is there for the art."

Ambrosia scoffed. "You're concerned about unsavoury company? I can only say—it's about time."

"Grandmama! You cannot hold the follies of my childhood against me forever," Felicia protested.

"A woman in her early twenties is hardly a child," Ambrosia said primly, "but you've matured nicely. Your marriage to Lord Davenport-Witt has done wonders."

"Grandmama!"

Charles chuckled. "It's quite all right, my dear. Your grandmother isn't entirely wrong."

"I understand Valentino is also going to show some of his paintings," Ginger said, "and did I hear something about auctioning them off? That is rather —well, peculiar, for an artist to sell his own work in that fashion."

"Precisely," said Charles wryly. "'Peculiar' is Valentino's watchword."

"I call that more than peculiar!" Ambrosia said with a frown. "And I don't understand. I thought you were going to a fancy dress ball at that Zouch-Nettleby lady's country house!"

"Yes, we are," Ginger said. "Lady Horatia is hosting the event, for Lucien Valentino."

"As for the fancy dress, that's another peculiarity," Basil put in. "No costumes like at a normal masquerade, just masks. I can't say I'm sorry that I won't have to dress up as Mark Anthony to Ginger's Cleopatra. Not that she wouldn't make a charming Cleopatra, but I dislike wearing a toga." He grinned at Ginger across the table.

Ambrosia sniffed. "Modern manners! I'm glad that I'll be safely at home and staying warm and dry. I always thought masquerades were tomfoolery, anyway."

"I think they sound like fun," Scout said wistfully. "I wish I could go."

Ginger smiled indulgently. "I doubt you'd enjoy it, son."

"So it's a masquerade cum art exhibition cum art auction cum New Year's Eve party," Basil said. "A rather unusual mix. Why the masks, I wonder?"

"As I said, 'peculiar' is Valentino's trademark," Charles said. "Perhaps he thinks that if he gets some sales, the masks will help the buyers remain discreet."

"As masks often do," Basil murmured.

"I suppose it adds to the allure," Ginger said, though a faint flicker of unease stirred at the back of her mind.

Outside, the wind whispered again, this time more urgently. The mantel clock chimed softly. Boss, sensing the close of supper, trotted to Ginger's side and nudged her hand.

"Come along, old friend," she said, rising. "Shall we move to the sitting room for coffee?"

As they made their way out, the house hummed with quiet contentment—and Ginger wondered if this peace could possibly last through the new year.

CHAPTER TWO

*T*he master bedroom at Hartigan House exuded the understated elegance Ginger Gold favoured—a harmony of soft creams, muted golds, and pale sage green. Heavy brocade curtains framed tall windows that overlooked the frosted gardens below, which gleamed wetly from the recent drizzle. A low fire crackled in the hearth, banishing the winter chill from the air. The large four-poster bed, its carved posts polished to a rich gleam, was draped with embroidered counterpanes and a mound of pillows. A set of gold and white striped armchairs snugged a small round table against the long windows, the perfect spot for morning tea. In the corner sat an old gramophone, a remnant from Ginger's days with her late husband, Daniel.

Lizzie stood beside the open wardrobe, carefully folding a shawl into Ginger's overnight case. A pair of low-heeled satin shoes, carefully wrapped in newspaper, had already been tucked beside the second gown, a more practical frock in case of muddy conditions. The Chilterns, after all, were notoriously tricky in winter weather—chalk roads that could become impassable after only an hour of steady rain. Lizzie had said as much with a pinch of concern as she laid out a small tin of salts and spare gloves.

"I wish you didn't have so far to drive, ma'am," she said now, pausing with a pressed chemise in her hand. "There's no station nearby. If the motor gets stuck, you'll have no one but the foxes to call for help."

"That's why we're taking overnight things," Ginger replied gently, buttoning her earrings at the vanity, "because we're spending the night. We'll be fine."

Lizzie gave a soft huff of disapproval but said nothing further. Instead, she carefully placed a folded cloak into the larger of the travelling cases and stepped back. "I've filled your flask with tea and just in case, I've packed extra hair pins."

"You think I'll lose my head?"

"I think you'll lose patience long before your head, Mrs. Reed."

Ginger laughed and reached for her hand. "Thank you, Lizzie. Truly."

At that moment, Basil entered from the adjoining dressing room, fastening his cufflinks. He was striking in formal evening dress—a black tailcoat with satin lapels, crisp white shirt, and ivory waistcoat. His mask, waiting on the dresser, was equally discreet: black, masculine, and modestly adorned, designed to obscure little but lend an air of mystery.

Lizzie gave a respectful nod and slipped quietly from the room, closing the door behind her.

"The belle of the ball, indeed," Basil said, taking in the sight of his wife in her pale champagne gown, her curls pinned and dusted with gold.

Ginger reached up, laying her hand over his as he approached. "Have you any more intelligence on Lucien Valentino, love? I know you wouldn't be able to resist a little quiet digging."

Basil's expression shifted slightly, the gleam of the investigator behind his eyes. "Only what anyone with access to the public record might find. Entirely above board, I assure you. Society pages, archived reviews, the usual."

"And?"

"Valentino," Basil began, adopting the measured tone he used when briefing a case, "born 1880 in Marylebone, son of a rather disreputable merchant banker and a French mother. Educated in Paris. Made something of a name for himself as a painter in Montmartre before returning to London around 1912."

"I vaguely recall hearing his name back then," Ginger murmured. She and Daniel had honeymooned in London in 1913. "Something about a party—an infamous affair that ruined the reputations of several young debutantes, if I'm not mistaken."

"Quite correct," Basil confirmed. "The scandal was muffled, of course—their fathers paid handsomely to keep names out of print—but the whispers were damning enough. Valentino has always danced along the edge of scandal. His talent shields him, to some degree."

Ginger sighed and reached for her gloves. "Which makes one wonder why we're attending at all."

Basil stepped around to face her, taking her hands gently. "Because we've accepted the invitation, and to decline now would cause more notice than to attend quietly. Besides," he added with a warm smile, "you'll be perfectly safe. And rather dazzling, if I may say."

"Flatterer." She smiled despite herself. "Though this mask will do nothing to hide my identity. Red hair isn't exactly subtle. Nor is being escorted by Scotland Yard's own Chief Inspector Reed."

"That, my love, is rather the point of a masquerade, isn't it?" Basil said, lifting her mask and holding it up to her face. "To pretend, for a few hours, that we are something other than ourselves—even though everyone knows precisely who we are."

Ginger studied his face, the strong jaw and steady gaze she trusted implicitly. "And you? Will your reputation as a man from Scotland Yard follow you in there?"

"I imagine so. But Valentino's sort aren't generally the ones dabbling in criminal matters of my department—at least not directly. He prefers society games."

"Still, something about him unsettles me." She glanced toward the window, where the rain was still drizzling down. "It feels like we're stepping into a den of wolves."

"Then let us make certain we don't appear like lambs," Basil said softly. "Besides, we shall have

Charles and Felicia with us. And if anything unto-
ward arises, I shall be at your side."

"Always," she agreed, her voice warm.

Before they departed, they made their way down
the corridor to the nursery. Rosa, already tucked
beneath a mound of blankets, stirred as Ginger
leaned over to kiss her forehead.

"Sleep well, my darling," she whispered. "Happy
New Year."

Basil softly kissed Rosa's cheek as well. "Be good
for Nanny Green, pet."

Rosa murmured something unintelligible and
shifted beneath the covers, already returning to her
dreams.

In the adjacent room, Scout sat reading a well-
thumbed volume on horse anatomy. His face lit up
as they entered.

"You both look smashing!" he declared, eyes
widening at Ginger's gown. "Let me see your masks."

Ginger and Basil slipped on their masks and
smiled at their son.

Scout grinned widely. "Those are the cat's
whiskers!"

"Thank you, my dear." Ginger tapped the edge of
her mask lightly with a gloved fingertip before
removing it. "And a very Happy New Year to you,

sweetheart. You'll stay up with Nanny and listen to the wireless, won't you?"

"Of course," Scout grinned. "I can't wait for when I get to come along."

"It'll happen soon enough," Basil said, ruffling his hair lightly.

They descended the curving staircase to the large entrance hall. The chandelier, which had been converted to electricity some years earlier, cast a soft glow from its many crystal drops. The clicking of their heels echoed rhythmically across the black and white chequered marble floor, softening as they stepped onto the Persian rugs of the sitting room. Ambrosia was there, dressed in a deep burgundy velvet gown, sipping her afternoon tea.

"Do enjoy yourselves," Ambrosia said with a gracious nod. "Though the whole affair still seems ridiculous to me, if you don't mind me saying so."

"I'd expect nothing else, Grandmother," Ginger said with a smile. "We shall report back in full. I'm certain the account will be quite tedious." She tugged on gloves at the elbow, wiggling her fingers into place. "Happy New Year."

"Happy New Year, Lady Gold," Basil added.

"And to you both," Ambrosia returned, adding

archly, "Do try not to get your names in the gossip pages."

"We'll do our best," Ginger laughed.

Their footsteps echoed softly through the marble-floored rear corridor as they made their way to the back entrance. Boss, from his spot in the warm kitchen, roused himself to greet them. The way he stared a Ginger, his round eyes pleading, his little stubble tail shimming wildly, tugged at Ginger's heart.

"Oh, Bossy, I feel like I've been ignoring you." She scrubbed his ears, then looked up at Basil. "Do you think Lady Horatia would mind?"

"You want to bring your dog?"

"Our dog, love, and yes. Boss loves to ride in the motorcar." She scooped him into her arms. "At least with him I know I won't be bored to tears."

Outside, Clement, the gardener, stood waiting beside Basil's polished green Austin, its brass fittings gleaming in the light of the quickly gathering dusk.

"All ready for you, sir, madam," Clement said, opening the rear door.

"Thank you, Clement," Basil replied, then opened the passenger door for Ginger and Boss.

As Basil rounded to the driver's side, Marvin, the stable lad, who was Scout's cousin, emerged from the small stables, wiping his hands on a cloth. He was a tall, sturdy young man, his features open and boyish despite his years. His voice carried a simple warmth.

"Happy New Year, Mr. and Mrs. Reed!"

"Happy New Year to you too, Marvin," Ginger called gently, leaning slightly from the window.

As Marvin stood in the glow of the carriage lamps, Ginger watched him for a moment. It saddened her that a blow to the head during an amateur boxing match a few years ago had left him with his faculties impaired. Friendless, save for Clement and the horses, he never seemed to mind his solitude, content to tend to the stables with tireless devotion.

At least, she mused, here at Hartigan House he was safe. And happy, in his way.

With a soft chug of the motor, Basil eased the Austin down the mews. Raindrops spattered gently as the house receded behind them. He circled back onto Mallowan Court, parked in front of the Davenport-Witt house and squeezed the rubber ball of the motorcar horn. Charles and Felicia, like Basil and Ginger bedecked in their evening finery, climbed into the backseat.

CHAPTER THREE

*T*he motorcar purred through the slick streets of Kensington, its headlamps slicing twin beams through the veil of drizzle that had enveloped the capital.

Ginger sat beside her husband, gloved hands holding Boss on her lap, her gaze drifting across the glistening terraced houses and shuttered shopfronts sliding past her window. Christmas garlands sagged over doorways, their greenery dulled by damp, while lamplight pooled in golden ellipses on the wet pavement.

They passed through Marble Arch, where the gas lamps hissed in the rising mist, then skirted the edge of Hyde Park, its skeletal trees stark against the darkening sky, black limbs laced with fog. London's fashionable west began to fray at the edges—ware-houses and brickworks replaced grand squares, and chimney pots stood like rows of watchmen along the rooftops. As the Austin carried them along Uxbridge Road, the last of the city's lights slipped behind them.

Soon, inside the snug cabin of Basil's Austin, the only sounds were the rhythmic click-thwack of the windscreen wipers and the hiss of the tyres on the rain-slick country road. The warmth of the engine was just enough to keep the windows from fogging entirely.

Behind them, Charles and Felicia sat in composed silence, the occasional jostle over a rut in the road drawing them shoulder to shoulder. They exchanged no words, but the stillness between them felt more companionable than strained. It was the kind of journey that demanded patience and diplomacy, both of which Felicia possessed in abundance when she chose to exercise them. "Well," Charles said at last, his voice cutting gently through the hush, "if this rain keeps up, we may need a boat."

"It's the wind I don't like," Basil replied. "The roads beyond Beaconsfield are chalk and clay—deceptively smooth until you lose traction on a corner and find yourself in a ditch with a wheel in the air."

"Let's hope the weather holds long enough for us to arrive with dignity intact," Ginger said, glancing at the horizon. Storm clouds were massing, bloated and dark, their bellies glimmering faintly with distant lightning. "I've no desire to be dragged out of a hedge in full evening dress."

Felicia gave a soft, dry laugh. "The roads will be passable," she said, her eyes still fixed on the land-scape beyond her window. "They always are—until they're not."

Her voice was even, but there was something in it —an old edge that stirred Ginger's instincts. She turned slightly in her seat, watching the rivulets of rain trickle down the glass. Something in Felicia's detachment felt like more than travel weariness.

The motorcar dipped gently as they passed through Gerrards Cross, and soon the fields opened up again—drenched and silvered in the glow of the headlamps, hemmed in by low stone walls and skeletal hedgerows. Puddles shone like black mirrors, and the wind pushed insistently at the Austin's frame, moaning faintly as they climbed.

"I read this morning there's another hunger march planned for January," Charles said, his tone measured. "Manchester to Westminster. Same route. Third one this winter."

Felicia's brow furrowed. "They'll freeze before they're heard."

"MacDonald won't act unless it's presented in Parliament with cigars and cufflinks," Charles said.

"Even then, he'd rather defer," Basil said. "Labour's talking reform, but no one wants to admit just how much the Empire is hollowing out."

"Not that it will stop Valentino's auction," Ginger said lightly. "Nothing like a bit of Continental-style decadence to take one's mind off industrial collapse."

"The contradictions of British society, as constant as rain," Basil replied. "One hand in velvet gloves, the other out for bread."

"I wonder sometimes," Ginger said softly, "if the whole country isn't wearing a mask."

No one spoke for a time after that. The only sound was the wet, rolling rumble of tyres on narrowing lanes, and the protest of the engine as the Austin began its ascent into the Chiltern Hills. The landscape grew more wild and brooding with every mile. Long ridges loomed, their slopes streaked with muddy tracks and empty copses that swayed in the rising wind.

Rain misted the windshield, then turned to

something heavier—a spatter of droplets that sounded like thrown grit. Basil leaned forward, adjusting the speed and squinting against the gloom. The car's lamps lit only what was immediately ahead: dark hedgerows, thick with leafless brambles, the glint of a half-flooded ditch.

"Careful here," Charles said. "We're getting close. If we go over the edge, there'll be no pulling out until spring."

Ginger felt the car shift under her, the tyres slipping ever so slightly as the grade steepened.

She glanced again at Felicia in the large rearview mirror. Her mask sat in her lap, her gloves neatly folded over it, her posture rigid. Beautiful. Controlled. Unreadable.

Felicia and Charles. Ginger had long suspected that neither had truly left the shadows of the war behind. Charles's charm was polished, effortless— but his silences were deliberate, the kind that came from watching, not weariness. And Felicia had come back from her war work different. Steadier. Sharper. It had been hidden under the "bright young thing" persona she affected for a lot of years, but it had always been there.

Ginger had seen it before. In mirrors. In briefings. In the faces of friends who never returned.

She herself had served with the Intelligence Corps—long days behind lines, long nights behind disguises. She knew how the Service worked: you didn't retire so much as fade, and even then, it was never quite clear whether the quiet ones were truly out—or just waiting.

A low groan beneath the wheels pulled her forward again. The motorcar went around a narrow bend, its headlamps catching the faint glint of iron gates half swallowed by hedges. The sign on the stone pillar read: Greystone Hollow.

Beyond it, the manor emerged from the fog. Pale stone walls streaked with lichen, high chimneys rising into the mist, ivy clinging to corners. A turreted wing jutted into a dark grove of trees, and light flickered through diamond-paned windows.

"Well," Basil muttered, guiding the Austin carefully under the porte-cochère, "we made it."

"Just barely," Ginger said. "Let's hope the house is warmer than the welcome."

She stepped out first, the wind tugging at her cloak, and cold rain stinging her cheeks. Boss whimpered in her arms, and Ginger wondered if perhaps the decision to bring Boss had been too impulsive. Behind her, Felicia adjusted her mask with gloved fingers and said nothing.

As the great oak doors swung open before them, the light spilling out and glinting off the driving rain, Ginger raised her chin, pushed her mask into place with her free hand, and crossed the threshold.

They were greeted by a young footman. "Allow me to take your bags to your rooms," he said, then efficiently carried the first load up the long staircase.

Lady Horatia Zouch-Nettleby's estate was a fusion of aristocratic tradition and avant-garde flair. Outwardly, the manor was in the most gothic style of the last century, but inside, the manor revealed itself to be built on a grand scale. A two-story hall rose before them, hung with ancestral portraits. High ceilings with ornate plasterwork loomed above, lit by crystal chandeliers that swayed faintly in the draught, casting shifting patterns across the marble floor beneath. The scent of beeswax polish and fresh-cut hothouse flowers mingled with expensive perfume and a whisper of cigar smoke.

In the drawing room, a fire crackled in the hearth, but it was the hush beneath the chatter that struck Ginger first—a tension, like an overture held one beat too long before the curtain rose.

A few guests had already begun to gather—a swirling kaleidoscope of velvet cloaks, feathered masks, beaded gowns, and dark tuxedos. Some masks were simple, others elaborate—horned, gilded, painted with grotesque expressions or romantic flourishes. Ginger noted that despite the intention of anonymity, the illusion was paper-thin. A man's stance, a woman's laugh, the shape of a jaw or the scent of a familiar perfume—one could still see what lay beneath.

"Quite the spectacle," Basil murmured, offering his arm.

"Lady Horatia has certainly spared no expense," Ginger replied, adjusting the edge of her gold-trimmed mask. "She always did enjoy her role as patroness and orchestrator of society's more indulgent affairs, even if they're on a small scale like this one."

As if summoned by her mention, Lady Horatia appeared, sweeping across the marble floor with theatrical poise. She was a tall, commanding woman in her early fifties, her hair cut fashionably short in a silver-touched auburn bob. Her gown—a flowing robe of deep emerald velvet—hung loose in the modern style, embroidered with dark beadwork that shimmered as she moved. Her mask was an exquisite fan of peacock feathers and emeralds, framing her sharp eyes.

"Mrs. Reed, Chief Inspector Reed!" she greeted

with unmistakable warmth, though her tone had the polish of performance. "Lord and Lady Davenport-Witt."

"It's so obvious?" Ginger asked with a pleasant laugh.

"Well, I recognised you—even a mask can't disguise impeccable posture and taste," Lady Horatia replied amiably. "And of course, darling, I know whom to expect. Happy New Year."

"Happy New Year, Lady Horatia," Ginger returned. She admired the hostess's gown. "You look lovely."

"And your gown is simply divine, my dear. A find from Feathers & Flair, I gather?"

"Naturally," Ginger said. Having her own Regent Street dress shop definitely had its benefits.

"Then I shall say no more—save that I expect you'll outshine every other lady here." Lady Horatia's eyes sparkled behind the mask. "But come! Pleasure and art awaits. Lucien Valentino has brought some truly remarkable pieces—one or two that may even stir a little scandal."

"I can't imagine anything more appropriate," Basil said dryly.

At that moment, a lean, narrow-shouldered man emerged from the side hallway, balancing a clipboard and murmuring instructions to a uniformed footman. His black velvet mask did little to soften his severe features or the irritation clinging to the corners of his mouth.

"Ah, and here we have the tireless steward of tonight's display," Lady Horatia added. "Endicott— Lucien's assistant, though I suspect he does more herding than helping most days."

Endicott gave a tight smile and inclined his head. "W-welcome."

"I look forward to the exhibition," Ginger said. "It's not easy making art behave."

"Indeed," Endicott said, glancing towards the windows. "P-particularly when the weather seems determined to be against us. I did not dare bring the watercolours, they would be ruined."

With a curt nod, he turned and strode off, issuing quiet orders as he vanished behind a pair of velvet curtains.

Ginger adjusted her mask. "Let's see who else is lurking behind the glitter."

*a*s they began to circulate slowly through the drawing room, Ginger could feel the tension humming beneath the surface. Conversations held a clipped, breathless quality, as though everyone was trying to speak through silk.

"Look there," Basil said, nodding subtly toward a tall, thin man in a raven-black mask. "That's Nathaniel Zane. Owns a fleet of merchant ships, among other things."

"Known for more than just shipping, if the rumours are correct," Ginger added quietly. "There are whispers he moves stolen art through the ports. Perhaps he's hoping tonight's acquisitions will make his private collection look more legitimate."

Mr. Zane was deep in conversation with a tall,

sharp-featured woman in a striking bronze mask shaped like a falcon's beak.

"That's Delphine Valentino," Basil said. "Lucien's sister. She used to be a ballet dancer with the Paris Opera Ballet."

"She walks like one still," Ginger noted. "And carries herself like a lady who's cleaned up after her brother more than once."

They continued through the drawing room, passing a dark-haired woman in a crimson dress, cut daringly low for winter. Her mask was a swirl of black lace and rubies under her feathered headdress, but Ginger recognised the calculated sweep of her glance.

"Lady Ione Partridge," Ginger murmured. "Twice widowed, thrice betrothed, and currently unattached."

"And wealthy again, for now," Basil said. "Though I suspect her interest in art is less academic and more acquisitive."

"Or romantic," Ginger said. "She's already appraising the eligible men like she's choosing which painting to hang over her mantel."

Basil raised a brow. "At her age?"

Ginger assessed the age of the woman in question to be in her late-fifties. "It's never too late to find love."

An attractive lady stood nearby, sipping champagne. Her mask was modest—powder blue silk trimmed with pearls—but she carried herself with the poise of someone raised among artists, diplomats, and discreet scandals.

"Mademoiselle Vivienne Brousseau," Basil said softly. "A well-known art dealer."

Felicia and Charles appeared at their side. Charles's tuxedo was immaculate, and Felicia's silver lamé gown shimmered beneath the chandelier light. Her mask was moonstone and frost—a perfect complement to her cool, hesitant expression.

"You seem uneasy, my dear," Ginger said softly, slipping an arm through hers.

Felicia offered a quick smile. "It's nothing. Just a bit of a ghost from the past."

"Anyone we should be concerned about?"

"No. Truly. Just... an old version of myself I'd rather not meet again."

Ginger was quite aware of Felicia's former flighty and immature antics, and had been much relieved, as was Ambrosia, when Felicia married and moved on from her devil-may-care ways.

Before Ginger could say more, a sudden voice rang out behind them.

"Ah! My honoured guests!"

Lucien Valentino swept into view, his brocade coat shimmered in gold and black. His mask was plain black, but his silver-streaked hair and hawkish gaze made it anything but unremarkable.

"Mrs. Reed, Chief Inspector Reed, Lord and Lady Davenport-Witt—how radiant you all look. Your arrival elevates the entire evening."

"Happy New Year, Mr. Valentino," Ginger said, offering a gracious nod.

"Happy New Year, indeed," Lucien said. "Tonight is a culmination of my latest creative efforts—drawn from my time in Vienna, Prague, and Berlin. Art is the only thing that tells the truth, wouldn't you agree? Money lies. Power fades. But beauty? Beauty endures."

"An optimistic view," Basil said mildly.

"Ah, Chief Inspector—optimism is the mark of true survival. Now, please—mingle. Explore. Let the art speak. And above all—enjoy the masquerade. It's not every night one gets to be someone else."

With a graceful bow, Lucien continued on into the room, the black folds of his coat flaring like wings.

Ginger exhaled slowly. "He certainly knows how to command attention."

"And manipulate it," Basil added.

There was a gramophone playing dance tunes at the side of the room. Ginger had expected more. A live band perhaps, or at least a musician at the pianoforte—after all, they had been invited to a masquerade, which usually meant a ball. However, given the small number of guests and the simplicity of the music, clearly the evening was much more about the art than the dancing.

Despite this, the drawing room had been transformed into a dreamscape of shadow and shimmer. Silver and sapphire drapes cascaded from the high ceiling, softening the sharp edges of cornices and alcoves. Candles in gilded sconces cast flickering light against the marble, while mirrored panels reflected the few dancers in whirling, shifting tableaux. The floor—a gleaming stretch of parquet—had been cleared for dancing.

There were fewer guests than Ginger had anticipated. The weather was likely to blame. Conversation buzzed around them—low and confidential beneath the mask of elegance.

"Do you notice," Basil said under his breath, "that everyone's eyes linger just a second too long on everyone else? As if trying to guess who's behind the mask."

"It's delicious," Ginger murmured, her voice edged with amusement. "Though, it's hardly a great puzzle."

As the gramophone music shifted into a waltz, Basil guided Ginger onto the floor and into a smooth turn. Her gown rippled like poured champagne, her mask catching the chandelier light as they joined the dancers.

To one side, Nathaniel Zane leaned against a column, his drink untouched. His eyes were locked on Lucien Valentino, who stood laughing near the gramophone, animatedly gesturing. When Mr. Valentino turned in Mr. Zane's direction, he raised his glass in mock salute, then drew closer. Mr. Zane's jaw tightened. Words were exchanged, sharp and low, and though Ginger couldn't hear what was said, it was clear that there was no love lost between them.

A few minutes later, Basil and Ginger danced past Mr. Zane, who was now speaking to Delphine Valentino, loudly enough that Ginger caught his meaning.

"Your brother's a parasite. He'll drain the last drop from anyone foolish enough to get close."

"Tell me something I don't know," Miss Valentino replied coolly, her gaze never leaving her brother.

"He hardly creates anything new anymore. He feeds off the memory of having once mattered."

Ginger raised a brow at Basil. "No love lost between the Valentino siblings."

Not far from them, Lady Ione Partridge danced with a younger man in his early forties in a dove-grey mask. She smiled—perfect, predatory—but when Mr. Valentino passed by and bowed with exaggerated flair, her expression turned glacial.

"Still making grand entrances, I see," she said loud enough to be heard. "How quaint."

Mr. Valentino only chuckled. "My dear Lady Partridge, it's not the entrance that matters. It's the exit."

Lady Partridge laughed. "Lucien, try not to trip on your own ego on the way out."

Ginger whispered in Basil's ear. "Do you know the man Lady Partridge is dancing with?"

"I believe that to be Dorian March."

"You do know everyone, don't you love," Ginger said with a smile.

"When you've been working in public service as long as I have, you hear things," Basil explained. "He's an art critic and a collector. I don't know much more than that."

A quiet young lady stood near the refreshment

table, spinning the stem of her champagne glass. Her mask had slipped slightly askew, revealing flushed cheeks and an expression of barely contained distress. As Ginger and Basil twirled by, Ginger caught the way Mr. Valentino's shadow fell across her, moments before he appeared beside her.

"Nola," he purred, placing a hand on her arm. "Why so shy? You'll never make your mark if you're always hiding behind taffeta and teacups."

Miss Plimpton gave a start and nearly spilled her drink. "I—I'm not hiding," she said, her voice pitched surprisingly high. "I'm observing."

"Then observe this," Lucien Valentino said silkily. "Tonight, I unveil a piece unlike any you've ever seen. It will make your theories blush."

He moved away quickly, leaving Miss Plimpton blinking rapidly and pretending to examine a tray of petit fours.

"He's cruel," Ginger said quietly. "There's always a bit of performance in every artist, but he seems to relish unsettling people."

"He's not just cruel," Basil replied. "He's clever. He knows exactly where to press."

As the waltz drew to a close, the dancers applauded politely, and Ginger allowed Basil to guide her toward the edge of the room.

"Your dancing is as sharp as ever, Chief Inspector."

Basil grinned. "I follow your lead, Lady Gold."

Boss had been obediently waiting by the side of the room, where Ginger had told him to stay when they started dancing. She picked him up and made her way to the young woman that Lucien had called Nola.

"Hello," Ginger said. "I'm Mrs. Reed, and this is Boss."

"Nola Plimpton, madam." The young lady tentatively reached a gloved hand towards Boss. "May I? He won't bite, will he?"

"He's as friendly as they come," Ginger said, warming to her.

"Boss is such a funny name for a dog," Miss Plimpton said, her voice high and childlike.

"It's short for Boston," Ginger explained. "He's actually an American dog."

"You brought him over on a ship?"

"I did. Boss thought it was a great adventure."

Miss Plimpton smile saddened. "Your dog is more well-travelled than I."

A round of laughter nearby drew their attention —Lady Horatia, holding court with a few of her guests, was retelling a story that seemed to be about

Lucien Valentino's disastrous debut at the Paris Salon. "And then he claimed the entire judging panel was 'artistically illiterate'—and stormed out wearing nothing but a dressing robe and a cravat!" she said, fanning herself dramatically. "The nerve!"

"I thought that was an improvement," said Dorian March. The man was slender, pale, and stylish in an understated, vaguely decadent way. His dark slicked back hair had a faint widow's peak, and he dressed in monochrome layers with the elegance of a silent film star. His mask did nothing to hide his blank expression, carved from disapproval. "Before he started playing the provocateur, Lucien was almost respectable."

"You knew him back then?" Ginger asked, stepping closer.

"Unfortunately," Mr. March replied, his voice clipped. "We studied together in Florence. He always mistook mockery for genius."

Mr. Valentino entered the drawing room just then, his black mask gleaming like obsidian. He put on a new gramophone record, this time a foxtrot, and several dancers resumed. Mr. Valentino bowed to Lady Horatia, ignored Mr. March entirely, and then turned toward Ginger and Basil with a theatrical smile.

"Care to dance, Mrs. Reed?" he asked, offering his hand with an exaggerated flourish.

"Alas, I've already promised the next one to my husband," she said sweetly.

"Pity," Mr. Valentino said. "I do so enjoy leading."

"I'm sure you do," Ginger replied, her smile never wavering.

He gave a brief, sardonic bow and disappeared into the crowd.

"He's certainly gathering admirers," Basil murmured, "but not the fond sort."

Ginger's gaze swept the ballroom. Every guest behind every mask seemed to be watching Lucien Valentino—some with fascination, others with disdain. A few, like Felicia, turned their eyes away entirely.

"I'm starting to think," she said softly, "that if anything unfortunate were to happen to Mr. Valentino tonight... we'd be spoiled for suspects."

CHAPTER FIVE

*T*he drawing room hummed with polite conversation and clinking glasses. Boss found an unoccupied arm chair with a comfortable cushion and curled into a ball.

Ginger scrubbed his ears. "I think the trip here tired you out, hey, boy?"

Leaving Boss to catch up on his sleep, she joined Basil in the hall by an alcove just off the drawing room's east side. The alcove was quieter, set apart by a pair of fluted columns and a velvet curtain pulled back. Within, the lighting was dimmer, warmer, as if to frame the work displayed.

The statue dominated the space.

It rose from a base of veined black marble, all burnished bronze and jagged angles. The sculpture twisted upward like a double helix, with protrusions—vicious spines—jutting out from the base and at unpredictable intervals. A hollow void gaped at the centre, surrounded by thorned flares that caught the lamplight with sharp, golden glints. Despite the polished metal, the form suggested something primal. Something unfinished.

At the base, a plaque read:

Ascension

Vienna, 1925

Lucien Valentino

Ginger stepped carefully around the piece, her heels whispering over the thick carpet. She tilted her head. "Oh mercy. It feels… combative."

"Violent, more like," Basil said, keeping a safe distance. "One wrong step and you'd need stitches."

"I wonder what sort of mind dreams this up," she murmured.

"Ask, and you shall receive," came a voice behind them.

Lucien Valentino stepped into the alcove, hands clasped lightly behind his back, his black mask pushed to his brow. "Ah, Ascension," he said, with the reverence of a man naming a child. "Do you like it?"

Ginger turned. "I'm not sure 'like' is the word. It rather resists being liked."

Mr. Valentino smiled. "Good. Then it's working."

Basil arched an eyebrow. "You created this in Vienna?"

"I did." Mr. Valentino stepped closer to the sculpture and ran a gloved hand along its outer curve, carefully skirting around the spines. "In the dead of winter. I was living in a converted brewery—no heat, barely enough light. But my mind was aflame. I had just left the salons and the sycophants behind. I wanted to make something pure. Something honest. Not beautiful, not polite. Something that hurt to look at, but made you feel nonetheless."

Ginger's gaze flicked to the void at the centre. "It looks hollow."

"It is hollow," Mr. Valentino said, delighted. "That's the point. The human soul—rising, contorting, climbing ever upward. But always with a core of absence. Of yearning."

Basil studied him. "And you call that ascension?"

Mr. Valentino's smile faltered for a moment—just long enough for Ginger to notice.

"Of course," he said, recovering. "Art is not meant

to soothe. It is meant to elevate. Even through suffering. Especially through suffering."

Ginger folded her hands lightly. "And was it suffering that inspired this?"

Mr. Valentino's eyes glittered beneath the mask. "Isn't it always?"

He turned toward them, theatrical now, voice low and confiding. "I had just survived a... setback. An illness of the heart, let's say. Vienna taught me that transcendence isn't won through comfort, but through fire. Every artist must pass through the flame. This—" he gestured to the sculpture, "—is what rose from mine."

From the drawing room, a distant laugh rang out, jarring in contrast.

Mr. Valentino smiled faintly. "Most people don't understand it, of course. They think it's crude. Unfinished. Dangerous."

"They're not wrong about the last bit," Basil muttered.

Mr. Valentino chuckled. "Dangerous, yes. But only to illusions."

He bowed then, the gesture sweeping but tinged with irony. "Now, if you'll excuse me. The masks may be lovely, but the egos beneath them require tending." He swept out of the alcove like a man exiting stage left.

Ginger reached for a slim exhibition catalogue laying on a sideboard. It was printed on heavy cream stock with gold-embossed lettering: An Evening with Lucien Valentino.

She flipped through the pages. Eight pieces. Eight descriptions. Each paired with a title and a brief, cryptic caption. But no mention of Ascension.

"That's odd," she murmured.

"What is?" Basil asked.

She turned the catalogue toward him, tapping the blank space between the introduction and the first lot. "This sculpture—Ascension—it isn't listed."

Basil glanced back toward the alcove as they moved back into the drawing room. "Oversight?"

Ginger shook her head slowly. "Lucien Valentino doesn't strike me as careless. If anything, he choreographs chaos."

Basil arched a brow. "So it's intentional?"

"Possibly. Or perhaps someone else pulled it."

The call came not with trumpets or fanfare, but with the sudden silencing of the gramophone.

A hush swept through the drawing room like the last breath before a plunge.

Endicott appeared in the archway, solemn as a mortician. His tone, devoid of inflection, sliced through the murmurs. "Ladies and g-gentlemen, if you would kindly make your way to the east gallery. Mr. Valentino is ready to b-begin the unveiling."

A ripple of movement followed—curious, cautious—as masked guests turned toward the tall double doors. Velvet whispered. Champagne flutes were quietly abandoned.

Ginger exchanged a glance with Basil.

"Here we go," he murmured, offering his arm.

She accepted it, eyes scanning the crowd. Near the wall, Felicia clung to Charles's arm, knuckles pale against the dull black satin of his sleeve. Nola Plimpton lingered near the refreshments.

The east gallery had been transformed. Tall oak-panelled walls gleamed under golden electric lights. The air held the scent of varnish and beeswax. Velvet-draped easels stood in a solemn arc, each shape concealed beneath heavy cloths—some tall and angular, others squat and square—an assembly of secrets waiting to be revealed.

Lucien Valentino stood at the center like a ringmaster.

He had changed into a darker coat, the black silk catching candlelight like spilled ink. His mask gleamed with fresh lacquer, but wild tufts of hair escaped the edges. The illusion of control was beginning to fray.

"Art," he announced, arms half-extended, "is truth, dressed in illusion. And tonight, dear friends, you will see yourselves—more clearly than ever before."

Nervous laughter stirred, but no one truly smiled.

Endicott stepped forward with his catalogue. "Item One. The Salt K-king."

He pulled the velvet cloth from the first canvas.

Gasps rose.

A harbour glittered with gold. Faceless dockworkers drowned in waves of coins, while a figure in a top hat lifted a single crate marked "Art" onto a lifeboat.

Nathaniel Zane gave a tight exhale. "I say, is that meant to be me?"

Mr. Valentino smiled. "It's a commentary on fortune and sacrifice. But if the shoe fits…"

Mr. Zane's fists clenched. Ginger caught him muttering to Lady Partridge, "Dash it all. I've seen housemaids produce better art."

"Item Two. Widow's Mantle."

A regal woman stood shrouded in five mourning

veils, each one bearing a fading silhouette of a man. In her hands, a bleeding bouquet.

Lady Ione Partridge's lips pursed. "Ah. This again. As I told you last time, it's marvellous, darling. I adore it." The angry glitter in her eyes belied her honeyed words.

"Item Three. The Critic's Mouth."

It was a painting of a man resembling Dorian March with a monstrous jaw devouring paint-brushes, torn manuscripts, and tiny, flailing human figures. A quill pierced his tongue.

Mr. March let out a sharp breath. "Lucien, you never could handle criticism like an adult."

Ginger cast a sideways glance at Basil, and muttered, "I sense a pattern."

"Item Four. The S-swan and the Chain."

A ballerina in perfect arabesque, her ankle shackled to a fractured mirror reflecting Lucien's face.

Delphine Valentino stared at it with cool detach-ment. Her arms crossed. She said nothing. "Item Five. Paper Wings."

A young lady in a schoolgirl's uniform stood at the edge of a burning stage, wings of pages with what looked like watercolour paintings stretched behind her. A shadow loomed in the wings.

Nola Plimpton made a choking noise. Her fingers trembled around the stem of her glass.

"Item Six. The Gilded P-peacock."

A masked ball unfurled in paint—at its center, a woman radiant and hollow-eyed, a golden peacock feather fan concealing a dagger.

Lady Horatia clapped politely, her lips in a tight smile.

"Item Seven, P-portrait of a Lady."

The young woman in the painting reclined on a velvet settee, its scarlet colour blazing against a deep plum background. In one languorous hand she held a cigarette in a long holder, whose smoke coiled upwards to catch a glint of light near her cheek, while the other was draped carelessly over the back of the couch. Her bobbed dark hair was styled in loose waves, kohl-rimmed eyes half-lidded in a look that hovered between challenge and seduction. She wore a silver flapper gown that glittered with bead-work, cut so short it fell well above the knee, with the strap sliding off the left shoulder so it barely provided coverage.

Charles frowned. "Felicia?"

Ginger could barely hear Felicia's voice, trembling with mortification. "I—I don't know... It was years ago, at a party in Chelsea. I didn't think. He said it was nothing—just a sketch. I was a fool."

A harsh rattle of rain hit the windows, like pebbles being thrown at the glass.

The lights of the chandeliers gave a hesitant pulse, like a gasp suspended in crystal, flickered again—then went out.

The room was plunged in darkness.

A bolt of lightning cracked the sky, freezing the room in a single jagged flash—startled masks, twisted shadows, frozen gestures.

A clap of thunder shook the room, then blackness again.

"Ladies and gentlemen, remain c-calm!" Endicott's voice rang out. A second flash of lightning caught the gleam of his spectacles. "Do not move!"

Ginger drew in a breath. "Perfect timing for Lucien's little opera."

Lady Horatia's voice rang clear. "Lights. There are extra candles and matches in the sideboard."

Ginger grabbed Basil's arm. "Over here."

They fumbled to a drawer. Ginger found a tin and lifted it to her nose. "Matches."

"I've got the candles," Basil said.

Ginger struck the match. Light bloomed. Slowly,

flames spread through the gallery—sconces lit, candlelight catching gilt and fear.

Guests shuffled uneasily as if their masks felt suffocating. The glamour had curdled into menace.

Felicia tugged her moonstone mask from her face. Her eyes were wide, the pupils dark pools in the candlelight.

"Felicia?" Ginger asked.

"I hate storms," Felicia whispered. "And I hate being stared at when I can't see who's doing the staring."

"You're not alone in that."

Lady Horatia moved steadily among them, offering calm in clipped tones.

Ginger leaned in to Basil. "Head count?"

He nodded. "No one has left."

Lucien Valentino emerged, cloak swirling, mask askew.

"Well," he said, voice taut, "what's a masquerade without a little darkness?"

CHAPTER SIX

*G*inger removed her mask.

Dorian March saw her and did the same. "Hardly worth the trouble now, is it?"

Suddenly there was another flicker, and the electric lights came up again.

Mr. Valentino cried out, throwing his arms wide. "Oh, confound it all. Let's not be poor sports. The fun is just beginning." He pressed his thumb down on the wick of the candle nearest him, snuffing the flame.

"If you think this is fun," Mr. Zane said, removing his mask as well, "you're mad as a hatter."

In seconds, the masks came off, tugged free,

tossed aside, forgotten. Only Lucien Valentino and Endicott kept theirs on.

"Very well," Mr. Valentino said. "I'm not about to let you dampen my mood." He waved a hand toward his assistant. "Endicott, you may begin."

Endicott stepped forward, catalogue trembling in his white-gloved hands. He cleared his throat, though the sound barely carried above the hush that had fallen over the gallery.

"Item One," he announced. "The Salt King. Oil on c-canvas. Vienna."

A low ripple stirred the crowd, and the guests edged nearer, drawn as if by gravity. Only the bravest leaned forward, peering at the canvas through narrowed eyes and clenched jaws.

Endicott's voice droned on, with an occasional stutter, as if he truly was conducting an auction, dutifully citing the dimensions, the palette, and the artistic influences—Schiele, Klimt, a shadowy Viennese collective Lucien Valentino claimed to have studied under, though no one had ever verified their existence. It all sounded more myth than memory. A self-fashioned gospel of genius.

Mr. Valentino lifted his chin, his voice slicing cleanly through the hush. "Shall we open the bidding at ninty guineas?"

Silence.

It hung like smoke. Guests exchanged uneasy glances, but no hands moved.

"One hundred?" Mr. Valentino offered, tilting his head.

Somewhere at the back, a guest coughed. A glass clinked too loudly onto a silver tray. A woman adjusted her glove with nervous fingers. Still, no bids.

"One hundred ten?" he said, smiling like a fox at the rabbits.

Lady Partridge leaned toward Nathaniel Zane. Her voice, low and swift, was lost to all but Ginger, who stood close enough to glimpse the sharp flash of her eyes, but she could not understand what he said. Mr. Zane's jaw tightened. With visible reluctance, he raised a hand.

"Fifty," he said. "Pounds."

Mr. Valentino's teeth gleamed. "Thank you, Zane. Do I hear fifty-five?"

Silence.

Endicott seized the moment. "Sold. Item One to Mr. Z-zane."

Ginger's eyes narrowed. Mr. Zane's expression was sour, defensive. A man buying his own humiliation off the public stage.

"Item Two," Endicott intoned. "Widow's Mantle. Oil on canvas."

A hush rolled through the crowd like fog across a moor.

Mr. Valentino didn't wait for the full description. "Shall we say fifty pound?"

Lady Partridge lifted her hand with elegance of an aging ballerina. Her lips barely curved. "I should hate to see her in someone else's drawing room," she said archly. "Fifty."

"Sold," Endicott confirmed, eager to move on.

The tension thickened.

"Item Three," he said. "The Critic's Mouth."

Dorian March let out a sharp bark of laughter. "Oh, very well, Lucien. It's certainly not subtle."

Mr. Valentino gave a theatrical bow. "Truth rarely is."

Mr. March stepped forward, staring down the canvas. "Fine. Thirty-five pounds. And don't bother wrapping it."

"Noted," Endicott murmured.

"Item Four. The Swan and the Chain."

Delphine Valentino did not move, but her knuckles whitened around her wine glass. Her face remained a mask of contempt.

Mr. Valentino's voice was quieter now, almost intimate. "Shall we begin at twenty-five?"

Delphine's posture remained rigid. "Let's be done with it," she said curtly.

"Sold."

"Item Five. P-paper Wings."

Nola Plimpton made a soft, wounded sound— half gasp, half sob. Her eyes shimmered. She raised her hand as if dragged by invisible strings.

"Twenty," she whispered.

"Sold," Endicott said swiftly, without meeting her eyes.

"Item Six. The Gilded Peacock."

Every eye shifted to Lady Horatia. Her expression did not waver.

"A hostess must support her artists," she said crisply. "Thirty-five guineas."

Mr. Valentino offered a mocking bow. "How gracious."

Endicott turned the page. "Item Seven. Portrait of a Lady. Oil on c-canvas. Circa 1923."

Mr. Valentino's voice rose again, pride laced with provocation. "A rare early work. One of my first muses."

Charles's voice rang out. "That's enough."

Mr. Valentino ignored him. "Shall we open

bidding at twenty guineas?"

Felicia stood frozen. Her lips parted, but no words emerged.

Charles leaned toward her. "Felicia—don't."

She raised her hand anyway. "Twenty-five."

Charles looked away, silent, jaw clenched.

"Sold," Endicott murmured, scribbling the bid.

Just as Endicott was turning the final page, Ginger's gaze wandered to a narrow alcove beside the velvet drapery. Something half-hidden behind a stack of unused frames caught the light.

She stepped over, curiosity quickening her pulse, and slid the top frame aside.

A sketch stared back at her—charcoal on cream paper, delicate yet arresting. The subject's bare shoulders and lifted chin radiated defiance, though a trace of sorrow lingered in the eyes. The likeness was unmistakable.

Vivienne Brousseau.

Before Ginger could take a closer look, a hand darted in and snatched the frame from her grasp. Mlle Brousseau stood there, cheeks flushed, clutching the picture protectively to her chest.

"Mlle Brousseau?" Ginger said gently.

Mlle Brousseau's lips tightened. "This eez not meant for deesplay." She turned the frame slightly, her voice crisp with her French accent. "Lucien drew eet years ago."

"And yet it's here—tonight," Ginger pressed.

Her nod was stiff. "Oui. Because Lucien eez a liar."

Across the room, Lucien Valentino caught Ginger's eye and offered a knowing half-smile, saying nothing.

Mlle Brousseau's answering scowl was sharp enough to cut glass.

And then—

For a second time that night, the electric chandeliers gave a stutter.

A flicker. A groan.

Darkness fell.

Gasps burst forth—quick, frightened.

A chair scraped backward. A glass shattered. Someone screamed.

Once again lightning split the gallery in an unholy flash, casting twisted shadows across the walls. The paintings loomed like revenants. Guests stood frozen in mid-motion—faces distorted, eyes wide.

Thunder cracked overhead.

Then silence. And darkness

CHAPTER SEVEN

With the help of candlelight, the guests retreated into the drawing room—so recently the stage for flirtation, snide remarks, and veiled cruelty. It felt fragile and airless, as though the tension had seeped into the very plaster and the dim flames of the hastily lit candles had sucked all the oxygen from the room. The storm outside had transformed into something elemental. Rain hurled itself against the tall windows in waves, and the skeletal limbs of the ancient oaks scraped and clawed at the glass with a sound like fingernails on bone.

A log split in the hearth with a sharp crack, throwing a burst of sparks onto the hearth. The flare of red and gold illuminated the uneasy faces gathered nearby. No one flinched, but everyone noticed.

The guests had withdrawn from the gallery in subdued clumps, masks discarded, and bravado fading. Conversations faltered mid-sentence or never started at all. Some stood stiffly by the fireplace, silently watching the flames. Others loitered near the French doors, as if waiting for a lull in the storm to flee through them.

Lady Ione Partridge hovered near the refreshments, listlessly picking at a tray of cheese straws with manicured fingers. Her peacock-feather headdress hung askew, and she didn't seem to notice. Dorian March stood with his back to the room, refilling his scotch with the slow precision of a man trying not to drop the bottle. Nola Plimpton was curled into a wingback chair, her regret at having come to this gathering clearly written on her face. A glass of champagne sat untouched on the table beside her, beads of condensation trailing down the stem.

"By golly, I need to leave," muttered Nathaniel Zane. His fingers fumbled with the buttons of his coat. "I can't stay here. This is ghastly."

"You will never make eet," came the reply from Mlle Brousseau. She stood near the window, clutching the curtains in one gloved hand. "Zee road eez barely a road een daylight, let alone under that." She gestured at the rain streaking down the windowpane.

"Can't someone telephone for—for—an electrician or something?" Miss Plimpton' asked, her voice as brittle as spun sugar. She clutched her gloves in both hands, twisting them so tightly her knuckles turned white.

"I've been informed that the telephone lines are down, as well," Lady Horatia said. "The storm has brought them down somewhere near the crossroads."

The silence that followed was thicker than the air. Unease curdled into something heavier—dread. For a moment, even the fire seemed to retreat, its flames withdrawing from the edges of the grate.

Then, from the corner near the fireplace, the grandfather clock began to strike.

Bong.

Heads turned.

Bong.

Bong.

Midnight.

Bong.

No one counted down. No one clinked glasses.

Just eerie shadows in the light of many flickering candles.

Bong.

The windows shuddered as the wind howled harder.

Bong.

Vivienne Brousseau sat rigid at the piano bench, her back perfectly straight, her hands clasped in her lap. Her lips moved, but no sound escaped.

Bong.

Felicia drew close to Charles, her expression unreadable. His arm settled protectively around her waist.

Bong.

Ginger felt Basil shift beside her, his posture sharpening.

Bong.

Dorian March's voice—low and clipped—cut through the tension: "Here's to 1929."

Bong.

Lady Partridge spoke, sardonically, "Let's hope the year ends better than it started."

Bong.

Bong.

The final chime hummed away into silence.

Lady Horatia stood near the mantel, motionless,

her complexion waxy in the flickering firelight. Her hand reached slowly for the crystal decanter. She poured herself a generous measure of brandy, her movements mechanical. With one hard swallow, she drained the drink, then set the glass down.

It struck the marble with a hollow clink.

"We must all remain calm," she said, her voice strained but still clinging to authority. "There's no reason to panic. The staff will light more candles. The electricity—"

A windblast rattled the windows blowing the shutters open and with a crash, the drawing room door swung open wide.

Lady Partridge, who had stepped up next to Lady Horatia to reach for a drink, stared through the open door into the hall.

And then—she froze.

Lady Partridge's gaze locked on the alcove. For one long heartbeat, she did not speak. Her expression shifted from confusion to horror.

Her glass slipped from her hand and shattered on the hearth with a piercing crash.

"He's dead!" she cried out. "He's dead! Oh God—he's dead!"

The tension in the room snapped, and there were loud gasps and outcries.

Ginger headed towards the alcove.

"Lady Horatia—" Basil began.

But their hostess was already moving, weaving between the stiffening knots of guests. Basil was at her side in an instant, matching her pace.

The velvet curtains hanging from the entrance to the alcove were still tied back. The candles in the sconces on either side sputtered wax.

And there, beneath the twisted bronze monstrosity Lucien Valentino had named "Ascension", lay its creator. Lucien Valentino's body was dropped across the marble plinth like a grotesque embrace. One leg bent beneath him at an unnatural angle, as though he'd collapsed mid-stride.

And from his back, the tip of a jagged spine of the sculpture's base protruded where it had pierced his chest, straight through the heart.

Blood ran down the marble base, painting the golden sheen of the bronze black in the candlelight. It pooled at the base of the sculpture, soaking into the carpet. Drops clung to the twisting bronze, frozen in place.

Mr. Valentino's face was a mask in its own right —his lips drawn back in a snarl of death, the eyes staring upwards in an expression of shock—but also of something else.

There was an expression of wonder in those staring eyes.

It was as if in his last moment, Lucien Valentino realised that the curtain had fallen—and the final act had begun without him.

There was no doubt that he was dead. Nevertheless, Basil crouched beside the body, fingers pressing lightly to Mr. Valentino's throat.

He waited a moment, then looked up and gave a slow, certain shake of his head.

"He's gone."

Ginger didn't reply. Her eyes were locked on the scene before her—the sculpture, the blood, the twisted limbs, the expression that didn't quite make sense.

Behind them, chaos had erupted.

A chorus of gasps. Scattered cries. The sound of Miss Plimpton sobbing, of Lady Partridge demanding answers. Somewhere back in the drawing room, glass shattered. Vivienne Brousseau gasped. Dorian March swore.

But Ginger didn't turn.

She stood frozen, staring down at the man who had made himself the centre of every room.

Lucien Valentino, darling of scandal, illusion, and spectacle, had taken his final bow.

CHAPTER EIGHT

*G*inger pressed a hand to the windowpane next to the front door and peered out into the darkness. The glass was cold, slick with condensation. From the end of the drive, she could see two swaying pinpoints of light approaching—the storm lanterns Basil and Alfred, one of the footman, carried. As they came close to the house, she could see in the gloom of the lantern light how Basil's coat snapped against his legs. The young man beside him staggered and slipped in the mud, his cap lost in the gale and his hair plastered to his skull.

The front door banged open, carried on a burst of wind and dead leaves, and both men stumbled inside, dripping rain and panting with exertion.

Alfred looked utterly spent, his boots mud-covered halfway to the knees. Basil peeled off his sodden hat and removed his overcoat with difficulty, water puddling on the marble floor beneath him.

"Come down to the kitchen," Ginger said, "they'll have towels there."

Rain drummed against the leaded windows as Ginger followed the men down the service stairs to the working area of the house. The plush hush of the main rooms gave way to the utilitarian clatter and creak of the servants' space. The air smelled of coal dust, damp wool, polish, and pipe smoke, and the warmth of the cooking fires rose up the stairs towards them. The gas sconces along the tiled walls hissed and guttered, their light uneven and nervous.

The stairs came down into a vestibule near the kitchen entrance.

Jones, the butler, stood nearest the gleaming black range, a tall, spare man whose black coat seemed to hang on him like an extra shadow. His iron-grey hair was neatly parted, his expression one of measured patience. Beside him, Mrs. Pell—broad of shoulder, brisk of manner—wore a starched white apron already dusted with flour, a wooden spoon protruding from the pocket. On the wooden settle near the pantry door sat Betty, a fresh-faced under-parlourmaid with hair the colour of new wheat, her nervous hands pleating the edge of her apron.

Mrs. Pell stood in tight conversation with Jones. Alfred the sole footman, stopped beside them, wringing water from the ends of his sleeves. Betty stood back, a look of bewilderment on her face.

Mrs. Pell looked up, took in the state of Basil's and Alfred's clothing, and darted down the hall, returning with a stack of clean towels.

"Thank you," Basil said, passing one to the young footman, and began to dry his head and hands.

"Chief Inspector Reed," Jones said quickly, straightening as if caught in some dereliction of duty. "We were just reviewing the situation."

"Then let's review it together," Basil replied, his voice brisk. "We need a clear picture of what we're up against."

Mrs. Pell, who up to now had looked composed to the point of severity, was pale. Her hands twisted the hem of her apron as though she might wring truth from cotton. "The telephone is out, sir. We tried the exchange the moment the lights flickered, but all we got was static. Nothing since."

"And the line hasn't come back?" Ginger asked.

"Dead as a coffin nail," the housekeeper

confirmed. "We tried the parlour set, the library line, even the wall box in the hall. Nothing."

"The way out is impassable," Basil added. "Alfred and I checked."

"That's right," the footman said, still catching his breath. "The drive is a foot deep in mud, and the road past the main gates is even worse."

"I tried to shift the Austin myself," Basil said to Ginger. "The wheels spun like mad. The drive's turned to soup."

Alfred nodded. "I went out on foot after that, took the torch and tried the road past the orchard." He shook his head, shivering. "It's a river. Mud past the calves. Nearly lost a boot, and the lantern."

"What about the stables?" Ginger asked, glancing toward the rear of the house.

"The horses are dry, ma'am," Alfred replied, "but they're agitated. And no footing. They couldn't get through either, and the carriages are hopeless."

Basil turned to Jones. "Have you got a wireless in the house?"

"It's only a receiver, sir, for listening to the BBC, not something we could send messages out with." The butler made a helpless gesture. "And even if we did, between the stone walls and the interference from that storm, we'd not get through."

"No vehicles. No horses. No communication," Basil said grimly.

Ginger drew in a slow breath, then lowered her voice. "The person who killed Lucien Valentino is still inside this house."

Basil turned to the staff. "No one is to leave—guest or servant—without my knowledge and permission. If anyone attempts it, stop them and report to me at once."

Jones nodded. "Yes, sir. We understand."

"We need to keep morale up," Ginger said, shifting her tone toward calm reassurance. "Fires in every common room. Oil lamps and candles wherever needed. Plenty of tea on hand always. Light food—soups, sandwiches, finger things. And serve it as if nothing is amiss."

"A touch of order helps stave off panic," Basil added. "Routine is armour."

Mrs. Pell pulled herself a little taller. "Yes, sir."

They turned to go, but Alfred spoke suddenly, his voice uncertain.

"Begging your pardon, sir—madam—there's something else."

Ginger paused. Basil turned back.

Alfred's face was pale and strained. He shifted nervously, glancing at Mrs. Pell before continuing.

"This afternoon, just before the first guests arrived, I saw Mr. Endicott carry a parcel to the coach house. A picture. Wrapped in brown paper and tied with twine."

Ginger's brow furrowed. "You're certain it was a painting?"

"Aye," Alfred nodded. "Quite certain. I've helped move enough of them for Miss Brousseau to know what they look like."

"Was it labelled?" Basil asked.

"No, sir. Nothing on it at all. Just the string."

"Did you see him return?"

"No, sir. I didn't think much of it at the time."

Basil and Ginger exchanged a look.

"Keep this between us for now," Basil said. "Not a word to anyone—guest or staff."

Alfred nodded solemnly. "Yes, sir."

As they turned back to the main floor, Ginger paused at the foot of the stairs. The gas lamp flickered and flared again, casting their shadows long and uncertain against the wall. Somewhere overhead, a floorboard creaked—too heavy for a cat, too soft for confidence.

Ginger laid a hand on the rail and looked back at Basil.

Basil gave her a weary smile. "Let's see if we can make it to sunrise without another body."

The light above them hissed and dimmed. The storm clawed again at the windows.

AT GINGER'S FIRM SUGGESTION, Lady Horatia had ushered the guests back to the drawing room with clipped commands and a thin smile that brooked no argument. Their murmurs faded down the corridor, swallowed by the plush carpets and the banshee howl of the storm. The heavy doors clicked shut behind them, leaving the gallery hollow, cavernous.

Lucien Valentino's body still lay sprawled beneath his sculpture. His once-glossy hair was matted with blood, his elegant mask now skewed beside his cheek.

Charles and Felicia lingered near the wall, pale and stiff.

"Could he have stumbled?" Felicia asked, her voice quiet, uncertain. "He'd had quite a lot to drink."

Ginger stepped closer to the sculpture's plinth, lifting the hem of her skirt to avoid the dark smear pooling beneath Mr. Valentino's skull. The statue above loomed, its vicious spikes casting monstrous shadows that danced in the candlelight. It gleamed with cruel indifference.

But it was the base that caught her attention.

"Basil," she said softly.

He joined her immediately.

"There," she pointed.

"There's a kink in the rug. A ripple in the weave."

She carefully lifted the edge of the ornate carpet.

Beneath it, stretched taut across the floorboards, was a thin black wire. Barely thicker than twine, but unmistakably under tension.

"Tripwire," Basil confirmed grimly.

"Angled just so," Ginger said, studying its trajectory. "To catch the heel. Or the edge of a shoe. One sudden jolt and he fell forwards—directly into the sculpture. That spike is placed exactly at torso height."

"An installation turned execution," Basil said.

"And theatrical to the end," Charles added. "Lucien always believed art should disturb."

From the corridor came the soft rustle of skirts. Lady Horatia appeared in the gallery doorway, a cloth-wrapped parcel in her arms, her expression composed but grim.

"You asked for a camera," she said.

Basil stepped forward as she unwrapped the

bundle—a Zeiss Ikon Icarette, with black leather bellows and polished chrome fittings, and a brass-legged tripod. He accepted it with a nod of gratitude.

"It belonged to my late husband," she added, quietly. "It's fully loaded and has a roll of film in it."

Basil nodded and stepped back to the centre of the gallery.

He set the camera gently on a chair, opened the case, and folded down the front panel. Then, carefully, he extended the bellows and pulled the lens standard forward along the rails until it locked into position. Then he attached the camera to its tripod. He checked the focusing knob, adjusted the bellows tension, and confirmed the aperture—likely around $f/8$ to account for the low interior light, Ginger thought to herself.

Then he cocked the shutter with a small lever, checked the settings for a slow exposure—perhaps 1/10th of a second, given the flickering candlelight —and carefully composed the first frame, moving the tripod into position, peering down through the ground-glass viewfinder.

The shutter snapped with a soft metallic tick. A sound far too gentle for what it recorded.

Basil wound the knob on the film spool inside

the camera until the next frame number appeared in the red window at the back.

He circled the room slowly, documenting: wide shots of the gallery, the sculpture, the rug, the smear of graphite. Then close-ups of Lucien's body, the angle of the impalement, the tripwire.

Each photograph captured not just a scene, but a truth sealed in time.

Basil took the last picture. "That's it for the film."

Alfred appeared in the doorway, eyes wide and hands twisted at his sides. Dorian March followed behind, expression sombre.

"Shall we move him?" Mr. March asked.

Basil sighed. "Ideally, we leave the crime scene untouched until the authorities arrive."

Mr. March protested. "That could be hours from now. He'll certainly start to smell."

"We can move the body to the kitchen's cold room," Alfred offered. "It's the only place that'll keep until help can arrive."

"Very well," Basil conceded. "But do be careful. I'd rather not add any posthumous bruising."

Mr. March and Alfred laid out a length of linen canvas. Basil and Charles carefully pried Mr. Valentino's body—now beginning to stiffen—off the statue. It took the four men to lift him onto the linen. After swaddling the body in clean folds, Alfred opened the side door to the servants' stairs, and the four men disappeared into the hush beyond.

Ginger stepped forward, lifting the camera on its tripod.

She composed another frame: the plinth now bare of its occupant, the glint of wet blood, the echo of violence still thick in the air.

Click.

The shutter snapped again.

"A ghastly way to bring in the new year," Felicia murmured as she joined her.

"Indeed," Ginger said.

"I suppose one can be surprised by poor weather in the dead of winter," Felicia continued, more to herself than anyone. "But surely the storm will pass."

"One can hope."

Ginger began to circle the sculpture again. The light glinted off something near the pedestal's edge —a small flash tucked beneath the curve of bronze and blood.

She knelt.

Using the little tweezers she carried in her beaded reticule, she delicately retrieved a small, glinting object.

A tie clip. Silver with onyx inlay, the stone cracked clean through. Blood marred the clasp.

"Not Lucien's," she murmured. "Too plain. Too conventional."

She turned it over. Initials were engraved using a heavily flourished ornamental hand.

Basil returned, and she handed the tie clip to him. "What's this?"

"I found it beneath the pedestal."

"It's hard to make out."

Ginger agreed. "Possibly N.Z.?"

"Nathaniel Zane?" he said, arching a brow. "That feels... almost too convenient."

"I agree," Ginger said.

"Do you think it's a plant?" Felicia asked, stepping closer.

Ginger tilted her head. "Too early to tell. It's possible someone wanted it found."

Ginger stared back at the sculpture—once a monument to Lucien's ego, now his tombstone. She reached out and laid one hand against the cold bronze of the base. The metal had lost its theatrical gleam. Now, it just felt heavy.

"Lucien Valentino wanted a spectacle," she said quietly. "He built a stage to shame others. But someone else rewrote the script."

Basil pointed the camera one last time. He adjusted the focus, tightened the aperture to capture sharper detail, and aligned the frame.

Tripwire. Bloodstain. Graphite smear.

Click.

"Let's hope," he said, winding to the next frame, "they left more behind than just blood."

Outside, thunder cracked.

And somewhere in the house, Ginger mused, a killer waited for the next cue.

CHAPTER NINE

*T*he drawing room had fallen silent. Only the occasional snap from the fire broke through the oppressive hush. The storm still hurled itself against the tall windows in relentless gusts, making the leaded glass flex and groan in protest.

Ginger stood near the hearth, arms lightly crossed, her eyes quietly scanning the room, taking in every breath, glance, and posture. Each person had claimed a seat or solitary corner—none sat too close to one another, as if proximity might invite suspicion.

Lady Horatia had reclaimed her usual position on the tufted velvet chaise, one hand curled tightly around a brandy glass. Her coiffure had begun to loosen, tendrils of grey-streaked auburn escaping their pins. Pale beneath her rouge, she remained imperious, chin lifted as though daring anyone to suggest she was frightened.

Mr. Endicott, Lucien's long-suffering assistant, perched stiffly on the edge of an armless chair near the piano. He looked as though he might fold in half at any moment, lips pressed in a tight line, his catalogue clutched like a holy text.

Delphine Valentino stood rather than sat, arms folded, one hip resting against the console table. Her expression was unreadable, her movements controlled. But her eyes—dark and narrowed—swept the room like searchlights, flicking from face to face. Seeing as she was Lucien's sister, Ginger found her lack of outward grief more than curious—it was conspicuous.

Mademoiselle Brousseau sat low in an armchair near the fire, shoulders hunched inward. Her cheeks were blotchy, her lips pressed together to hold in whatever storm of emotion threatened to escape.

Dorian March slouched elegantly into a wing-back chair, one leg slung over the other. His fingers drummed a careless rhythm against the armrest, the picture of ennui. Ginger suspected it was mostly affectation—but not entirely.

Lady Ione Partridge sat upright on a low settee,

surveying the room. Her fan flicked open and shut in rhythmic disapproval, though the glint in her eye suggested she found the drama more stimulating than shocking.

Nathaniel Zane stood apart from the others by the sideboard, his back to the drinks tray. One elbow rested casually on the polished edge, but the fingers wrapped around his whisky glass were white with tension. His gaze moved constantly—from fireplace to guest, guest to window, window to door—never resting for more than a heartbeat.

Felicia and Charles were seated side by side near the hearth. Felicia's face was pale but composed, her gloved hands folded tightly in her lap. Her husband sat straight-backed, his expression unreadable, the firm line of his jaw betraying the effort it took to maintain it.

Basil stepped forward.

"Thank you all for assembling so promptly," he said. His voice was steady, the kind that invited attention without demanding it, but it carried an unmistakable edge of command. "By now, you are all aware of the situation. Lucien Valentino is dead—killed in a violent and deliberate manner. Based on what we know, we believe the murder occurred shortly after midnight."

He let that settle. The fire crackled again, spitting a sharp hiss into the silence.

Basil moved to the centre of the room. "Due to the severity of the storm, no one is able to leave the estate. Every motorcar on the property is stuck fast, the lane to the village is impassable on foot, the horses are stabled and unusable, and the telephone lines are down. The earliest we can expect any outside contact is once the storm abates—possibly by morning."

A visible ripple passed through the group. Mr. Zane's fingers clenched tighter around his glass. Mr. March rolled his eyes just enough to register disdain. Lady Horatia said nothing but sipped from her glass in a manner that suggested she had expected nothing less than disaster.

Basil took a breath. "Allow me to introduce myself more formally. I am Chief Inspector Basil Reed of the Metropolitan Police. Some of you may know this already. For the rest of you—now you do. I am treating this as an active murder investigation."

Ginger's gaze shifted to her husband. She had seen him in this role before—measured, firm, methodical—but it never failed to impress her how swiftly the warmth in him could give way to steel when duty required it. He did not posture, as some men might. He simply commanded, with quiet certainty, like a man who knew that the next several hours might uncover rot beneath silk.

"The body of Mr. Valentino has been moved to a safe location," Basil continued. "Until we can reach the local constabulary and a doctor, the alcove off the drawing room is to be considered a restricted area. It's not to be touched, approached, or disturbed for any reason."

Lady Partridge snapped open her fan with a sound like breaking parchment. "I assume, Inspector, this means we are all suspects?"

"I'm afraid so," Basil said coolly. "Someone in this house committed murder."

Miss Valentino let out a short breath that might have been a laugh, though there was nothing amused in it. Mr. Endicott turned a shade paler as he gripped his catalogue. Lady Horatia calmly finished her brandy and held out her empty glass as though expecting it to be refilled.

"I will begin conducting interviews shortly," Basil went on. "To assist me, I have asked my wife, Mrs. Reed, to participate. She is principal investigator at Lady Gold Investigations in London and has frequently assisted the Metropolitan Police on active cases. Her discretion and records of success speak for themselves."

All eyes turned to Ginger. She met them steadily. Some, like Lady Partridge's, were appraising. Others —Miss Plimpton's, Endicott's—held uncertainty, even fear.

"How very modern," Lady Partridge murmured, folding her fan with a click.

Basil ignored the comment. "You may move about the public rooms of the house—but the gallery, the alcove, and the telephone rooms are off limits, as are the rooms on the second floor.

"But my personal effects are up there," Lady Partridge said.

"As are mine," Mr. March added.

Miss Plimpton huffed. "Not all of us were given rooms."

"Nevertheless," Basil continued, "anyone attempting to enter these spaces will be considered obstructing the investigation. That includes guests and staff."

"Are we to be searched?" Mr. March asked, tone dry as dust.

"If necessary," Basil replied.

"I should like to c-contact a s-olicitor," Endicott said tightly.

"You may do so," Basil said, "when the telephones are restored."

Endicott opened his mouth as if to object further, then appeared to think better of it.

Basil turned toward Ginger and gave the smallest of nods. "We'll begin with Mr. Zane."

Mr. Zane raised his eyebrows. "Naturally."

Ginger stepped forward, her voice even. "If you'll come with me, Mr. Zane?"

Mr. Zane knocked back the remainder of his drink in one swallow, set the glass down with more force than strictly necessary, and walked past her without a word.

Ginger paused at the threshold of the drawing room, then glanced back at the assembled faces.

The fire popped again. A draught from the hall stirred the candle flames.

She met each gaze in turn—prideful, frightened, closed—and thought: The masks may be off, but none of them are done hiding.

CHAPTER TEN

*T*he study had been cleared and rearranged, two chairs facing each other in the centre of the rug. The intimacy of the space had taken on a cooler air—one of cross-examination.

The door opened and Nathaniel Zane entered with the rigid bearing of a man holding himself in check. His jaw was set, his shoulders tight beneath a charcoal dinner coat. He glanced between them, his eyes flickering briefly to the fire, then to the chairs, before resting—warily—on Ginger.

He didn't move to sit until Basil gave a small nod toward the empty chair.

"Mr. Zane," Basil said. "Please."

Mr. Zane lowered himself into the seat with controlled care, resting his palms on his thighs.

Ginger remained standing. "You purchased 'The Salt King' at the auction," she said without preamble.

"I did," he replied.

"You seemed reluctant," Basil added. "Or shall we say—resentful."

Mr. Zane's jaw tightened. "Reluctant, yes. Resentful, certainly. But not murderous, if that's what you're edging towards. Besides, I was hardly the only one to make a purchase."

"Let's begin with your relationship to Mr. Valentino," Basil said. He pushed aside a paperweight and a letter opener to make room for his elbows. "How did you know him?"

Mr. Zane leaned back slightly, folding his arms. "We met some years ago, at a private sale in Knightsbridge. He'd just returned from Vienna, full of talk about existential texture and Balkan technique. I found him insufferable, but compelling. He had a knack for getting noticed."

Ginger studied Mr. Zane carefully as Basil asked, "Would you consider yourself friends?"

Mr. Zane let out a short, humourless laugh. "Lucien didn't have friends, I'm afraid. He had opportunities. You were either useful to him or you weren't."

"But you continued to associate with him," Ginger said. "Why?"

"Because he was brilliant," Mr. Zane said simply. "And because investing in brilliance is profitable, even when the man behind it is unbearable."

Ginger stepped to the desk, resting her hand lightly on its edge as she watched him. "Would you say you were business partners?"

"Of a sort," Mr. Zane said. "I helped fund an exhibition in Prague, and he provided exclusive access to some of his early works. I thought I'd acquired something valuable." He shook his head. "Turned out, he preferred to create chaos more than canvas."

"Did he owe you money?" Basil asked.

"No." Mr. Zane waved a hand dismissively, though his jaw remained tight. "He repaid me last year—though not without reminders."

"Were you aware of the nature of the exhibit tonight?" Ginger asked. "And that The Salt King would be included?"

Mr. Zane's jaw worked for a moment before he replied. "Rather, I suspected. He hinted. I asked him not to. He claimed it wasn't personal, that it wasn't about me or him—which, in Lucien's language, always meant it absolutely was."

"Did you argue with him tonight?" Ginger asked.

"No. I had no reason to before…" he flapped a hand, "…his big reveal."

Basil leaned in. "But you were angry then?"

"Rather! Chief Inspector, you don't depict a man —and a specific man at that, namely me—smugly watching people drowning in gold, and call it 'commentary' unless you're purposely trying to be antagonistic."

"Is there truth in it?" Basil asked quietly. "Have you profited from exploitive trade?"

"Steady on, sir," Mr. Zane straightened slightly, holding Basil's gaze for a beat too long. "My business practices are legitimate and beyond reproach." He glanced away, his eyes tracking the firelight as if searching for something in the embers.

Ginger and Basil shared a look. Then Ginger opened her handbag and carefully withdrew something small, wrapped in a handkerchief.

"We found this beneath the sculpture," she said. "Near where Mr. Valentino fell."

She unfolded the cloth to reveal the broken silver tie clip.. Ginger held it in the lamplight to show the engraved initials on the back: NZ.

Mr. Zane stared at it.

"Is it yours?" Ginger asked.

He paused, then shook his head. "No, madam. I've never seen that before."

"Your initials are engraved on it," Basil said evenly.

Mr. Zane's brow furrowed. "Then someone else shares my initials."

Ginger arched an eyebrow. "Are you suggesting someone forged a set of initials onto a tie clip and planted it beneath a murder scene?"

"I'm suggesting," Mr. Zane said slowly, "that it's not mine. I wear a chain pin. I haven't used a tie clip in years."

Ginger studied him for a long moment. "You didn't lose one recently? Change your style for the ball?"

"No," he said firmly. But there was something in his voice—less defensiveness than bafflement. He genuinely seemed unsettled. He added, "Like I said, any bloke could share my initials. Noah Zachary, Ned Zelly, what-have-you."

Ginger gave him a long, considering look.

"We'll hang onto it," Basil said. "In case you remember otherwise."

Mr. Zane gave a stiff nod but avoided looking at the object again.

Ginger thought it time to return to the question of motive. "Do you know anyone who might have had a reason to want Mr. Valentino gone?"

He chuckled dryly. "Everyone who ever had the misfortune of meeting him, perhaps?" When Ginger and Basil didn't smile he added reluctantly. "As much as I hate to say it, I have to put forward his sister, Miss Delphine Valentino. She hated him. I don't say that lightly. Miss Valentino was the only one he feared, even slightly. She used to cover for him—until she stopped. That was when he got truly vicious."

"In what way?" Basil asked.

Mr. Zane shrugged, but it was more guarded than casual.

"Threats. Private things hinted at in public."

Ginger and Basil exchanged a glance.

"Thank you, Mr. Zane," Basil said at last. "That will be all for now."

Mr. Zane rose stiffly, adjusted the cuffs of his jacket with practiced precision, and exited, closing the door behind him.

Ginger lowered herself into the empty chair.

Basil moved to the hearth, one hand resting on the mantel as he stirred the fire.

"He's definitely hiding something," Basil said, "but I can't tell if it's guilt or confusion."

"Could be both," Ginger murmured. "Or he's telling the truth and someone's playing a deeper game."

Basil nodded slowly. "Then we'll play it better."

He straightened. "I suppose we should speak to Miss Valentino next?"

"Yes," Ginger said as she got to her feet. "I'll go fetch her."

The drawing room was a portrait of mounting discomfort. The air was close and restless, thick with the mingled scents of woodsmoke, candle wax, and the sharp trace of spilled brandy—a perfume of exhaustion and impatience.

Lady Partridge let out a plume of cigarette smoke before tapping the last vestiges of ash in the ashtray.

Charles and Felicia stood apart near the hearth, with expressionless face, tactfully doing their jobs of observation.

"So are we to be kept like prisoners all night?" Delphine Valentino asked, her voice cold.

Before Ginger could respond, Charles spoke up, his tone tight. "No one leaves the common rooms

until the interviews are complete. Surely you understand the need for that, Miss Valentino."

"For everyone's safety," Felicia added, her voice
calm but resolute. "Best that we all know where the
others are, don't you agree?"

Miss Valentino gave a hollow laugh. "The only
thing threatening me at this point is boredom. And
excessive fatigue." She gave another pointed yawn.

"I daresay, it's safer than finding a second body in
the morning," Mr. Zane murmured, not looking up.

Lady Horatia's chin snapped. "Surely, there's no
danger of that. Especially, if we stay together."

"Are you really suggesting that one of us is a
murderer?" Lady Partridge said with a note of
disbelief.

"Who else could it be?" Mr. March challenged.

"I don't know," Lady Partridge returned. "Perhaps
a stranger came in unawares, or one of the staff had
had enough of the pompous a—"

Lady Horatia cut in with a click of her tongue.
"Lady Partridge is right. This is intolerable. The
investigation is going in entirely the wrong
direction."

"You haven't forgotten about the weather, have
you, Lady Partridge?" Felicia challenged.

"Certainly not, Lady Davenport-Witt," Lady

Partridge replied. She produced a cigarette and matches. "But there must be another explanation."

"Your protestations are for naught," Mr. Zane said. "Until the police can be summoned, we have no choice but to oblige the representative on hand by answering his questions." He grinned wryly. "And it's not a great ordeal, I can assure you."

"Who's next, then?" Dorian March asked, rubbing a hand across his tired face, before staring up at Ginger. "You've grilled the financier. Are we moving on to artists? Patrons? Hapless assistants?"

Eyes flicked from face to face. Muscles tensed. Delphine straightened slightly. Charles set down his glass. Lady Horatia lifted her chin. Even Miss Plimpton dared to look up from her agitated pleating of her skirt. A breath passed through the room—silent and collective—as though each person braced to hear their name.

In the corner, Endicott jerked awake. "What's that?"

"Mrs. Reed is asking for the next interviewee," Mr. Zane said lazily, not turning.

Ginger let her gaze travel deliberately around the room before settling at last on Delphine Valentino.

Miss Valentino sat half in shadow, her knees tucked beneath her in a way that suggested a younger version of herself—watching, waiting. Her mask still dangled from one wrist, the silk ribbon a loose loop around her hand. Her skin looked wan in the low light, though her eyes, lit faintly by the fire, were bright and alert.

When she met Ginger's gaze, something flickered behind them—resignation, perhaps, or calculation. She took a breath and stood.

"I suppose I'm next," she said plainly. "It stands to reason that you'd want to talk to the sister."

Her gaze flicked towards Mr. Zane. "In fact, I'm surprised you called on Nathaniel before me."

Miss Valentino began to cross the room slowly. Her shoulders were squared, her mouth set in a neutral line. She passed each guest with careful steps, her presence momentarily drawing their attention.

"Well," she said as she paused at the doorway. "Let's not keep the ghosts waiting."

Ginger opened the door for her, and together, they stepped into the corridor.

CHAPTER ELEVEN

*D*elphine Valentino walked into the study like an actress summoned to the stage—not startled, not reluctant, and certainly not grief-stricken. She entered with feline grace, her silk sleeves whispering softly as she moved, the faint scent of violets clinging to her as though she'd walked through a garden no one else could see. Her hair, pinned with unforgiving precision, had not loosened. Her eyes were dry, and her expression cool.

She didn't look like a lady in mourning.

Without waiting to be offered a seat, Miss Valentino lowered herself into the armchair across from Ginger with the easy poise of someone used to being observed. She crossed her legs slowly, one elegant ankle resting over the other, and smoothed an invisible crease from her skirt.

"You'll forgive me," she said, tilting her head, "if I don't pretend to be devastated by my brother's death."

Ginger said nothing, only studied her. Basil leaned forward slightly, hands loosely clasped.

"Miss Valentino, would you describe your where-abouts between the time the lights went out and the moment the body was discovered?"

"Certainly." She angled her chin, as if granting an audience. "After that atrocious auction—which I only endured out of familial obligation—I returned to the drawing room with everyone else. The drinks trolley was still set up. I poured myself something stronger than the company and remained there until Lady Partridge screamed."

"Did you return to the gallery at any point after the lights went out?" Ginger asked.

Miss Valentino shook her head once. "No. I'd seen enough."

"You seemed particularly... detached this evening," Ginger said, watching Miss Valentino's expression. "Even before the tragedy."

Miss Valentino's lips parted in a ghost of a smile.

"Detached? I prefer to think of myself as emotionally efficient."

Ginger waited.

Miss Valentino gave a quiet sigh. "Lucien and I have been in a state of disagreement since we were old enough to insult each other in Latin. We never stopped circling the same flame—we just learned to burn at different temperatures. He dealt in humiliation. I preferred discretion."

"Did he threaten you?" Basil asked gently.

Miss Valentino's eyes flicked to him, then away. "Lucien rarely threatened. That would have required honesty. He preferred revelation—at the worst possible moment, and to the widest possible audience."

"And was he planning to do so tonight?"

She turned her face toward the firelight. "Not to me. But I warned him not to display The Salt King. I told him it would spark something."

"Because of Mr. Zane?" Ginger asked.

"Because Nathaniel doesn't take kindly to being painted into a corner. Or onto a canvas."

Basil sat a touch straighter. "Did Mr. Zane say something to cause you concern?"

"Oh, no." Miss Valentino's tone was airily dismissive. "But his type doesn't give warnings. They deliver outcomes."

"His type?" Ginger prompted.

"Men who've spent their lives being told yes, Mrs. Reed. Certainly, you've met a few in your time. Besides, Lucien didn't use words to lash out—he spoke in oils. Hung it up like a trophy. Auctioned it with finger food." Her voice darkened. "That painting was a taunt, not a commentary."

Ginger let the silence stretch before speaking again. "So you believe Mr. Zane is capable of murder?"

Miss Valentino met her gaze squarely. "I believe he is capable of being cornered. And when men like him are cornered, they either lash out or disappear." She gave a cool smile. "And the road's washed out, isn't it?"

"Miss Valentino," Ginger started, "you bought one of your brother's paintings tonight. 'The Swan and the Chain'. May I ask why?"

Delphine blinked once, slowly, as though the question touched something she hadn't prepared for.

"Because," she said, voice quieter, "despite everything, Lucien saw things. Not just flaws. Fractures. Long before they splintered." She held Ginger's gaze. "He really was very talented."

Ginger nodded once in acknowledgment. She pressed forward. "Did you previously know of the painting that featured Lady Davenport-Witt?"

Miss Valentino's composure didn't falter, but the answer came slower.

"Yes," she said at last. "And I told him it was a mistake to present it tonight. Her station has changed since the time it was painted. Some things don't belong to the public."

"And yet," Basil said, "your brother made a career of exposing what was private."

Miss Valentino's smile sharpened. "And now he's paid for it."

A heavy silence settled over the room.

After a moment, Basil said, "Thank you, Miss Valentino, that will be all for now."

Miss Valentino stood without flourish. She offered Basil a brief nod—equal parts civility and command—and exited with the same grace she had arrived. The latch clicked softly behind her.

Basil exhaled and turned toward Ginger. "Well?"

"She very much wants us to focus on Mr. Zane. I wonder what she has against him, exactly?"

Basil stood and moved to the sideboard. He poured two fresh cups of coffee, handed one to Ginger.

"She said something that stuck with me," he murmured. "'Lucien revealed. At the worst possible moment, and to the widest possible audience.' That's not theoretical. That's personal."

"Perhaps she's been burned. Or maybe she watched someone important to her get burned—and she never forgot the lesson."

Basil took a slow sip, then looked toward the door. "Do you think it's possible that she's protecting someone?"

"I don't know." Ginger adjusted a sequinned hair pin. "I think tonight isn't just about revenge or shame. It's about the cost of being exposed. And someone in this house is still hiding something they'd kill again to keep buried."

"Indeed," Basil said. "I believe it's time to speak to the victim's assistant."

CHAPTER TWELVE

*T*he study door creaked open once more.

Endicott stepped inside with the cautious shuffle of a man unsure whether he'd been summoned for a reprimand or a reckoning. His coat hung limply from his narrow frame, and his spectacles—slightly askew—were misted over. He took them off, dabbed at them with a monogrammed handkerchief, put them back on, then folded the handkerchief with fussy precision, a mere shadow of his former efficiency, his fingers trembling just enough to betray nerves he hadn't yet voiced.

"Endicott," Ginger said, rising from her chair. "Do come in. Please—sit."

"Oh. Thank you. Yes. Q-quite." He navigated to the armchair Delphine Valentino had vacated and perched on the edge, spine rigid, as though afraid he might sink into the upholstery and be unable to climb back out.

Boss, curled at Ginger's feet, lifted his head and gave a low, rumbly growl.

Endicott flinched visibly. "F-forgive me," he murmured. "I'm not t-terribly fond of d-dogs."

"He's very fond of people who tell the truth," Basil said mildly, though the warning was unmistakable.

Endicott offered a tight-lipped smile. "Ah. A discerning a-animal, then."

"Mr. Endicott," Ginger began, her tone measured, "how long have you been in Mr. Valentino's employ?"

"Six years," he replied promptly. "Well—five y-years and ten months. I began shortly after the Mayfair gallery opened. He said my cataloguing was meticulous. 'Pedantically charming,' in his words." He gave a dry chuckle. "I chose to interpret that as p-praise."

"I'm assuming that assisting with tonight's event was part of your duties?" Basil asked.

"Oh yes. Absolutely. I helped choose the p-paintings, oversaw framing, supervised their transport, worked with Lady Horatia as to the d-display, arranged the easels..." He paused, then added with quiet bleakness, "Everything, in fact, except—"

"Except what, Endicott?" Ginger asked gently.

"The g-guest list," he said, glancing toward the fire.

Ginger and Basil exchanged a glance.

"You weren't responsible for the invitations?" Ginger asked.

"I was. At first. Lucien and I d-drafted a list together—eighteen guests. A carefully b-balanced mix: patrons, critics, society figures, a few... combustible elements. But three days ago, he threw it all out." Endicott adjusted his glasses with two fingers. "Said there'd been 'a shift in t-tone.' Rewrote the list by hand, sealed every envelope himself, and posted them without a word to me. When I asked, he said—" He paused, lips twisting in memory. "He said, 'Art is war, Endicott. And every g-general keeps a few secrets from the quartermaster.'"

"Curious," Basil said. "Did you press him further?"

"I learned not to," Endicott replied, weariness creeping into his voice. "Mr. Valentino adored misdirection. Especially when it p-put others off balance."

"Were you aware that he'd painted certain

portraits in secret?" Ginger asked. "Works not previously exhibited?"

Endicott hesitated. "Some. He c-called them his 'arsenal.' Said no one had asked for them—but everyone had earned them." A crooked smile. "He claimed they were pieces p-painted in self-defence."

"He wasn't joking," Basil said flatly.

"No," Endicott said, folding his hands. "I see that now."

"Did you know he intended to display the portrait of Lady Davenport-Witt?" Ginger asked.

Endicott's face lost what little colour it had. "No. Nor The Salt King. That painting—he locked it away in a cabinet at the gallery last week. I w-watched him padlock it myself."

"And yet it was here tonight," Ginger said.

"Then he must've arranged for its delivery separately," Endicott murmured. "Mr. Valentino had a courier he used sometimes. Anonymous. He liked s-secrets—even from me."

Basil leaned slightly forward. "One of the footmen said he saw you earlier this afternoon—carrying a wrapped canvas out toward the coach house. Do you care to explain that?"

Endicott froze. "I—I was merely safeguarding a p-piece," he stammered. "It was raining. I didn't want it left near the d-doors where the wind might damage it. Mr. Valentino would've been furious."

"What piece?" Ginger asked.

"I don't recall exactly," he said, shifting in the chair. "One of the unsigned ones, I believe. A sketch, not meant for v-viewing. He had instructed me earlier to keep certain works out of sight unless he called for them."

"And did he?" Basil asked.

"No," Endicott said quietly. "He never did."

"Then why move it at all?" Ginger pressed.

His mouth worked for a moment without sound. "I suppose he feared someone else m-might."

Ginger's eyes narrowed slightly. "Any idea who?"

Endicott swallowed. "I couldn't really say, madam. Perhaps Mr. March?"

"Why him?" Basil asked.

"They were very c-competitive." Endicott let out a long sigh. "Honestly, I didn't understand it. Mr. Valentino was in a completely d-different league than March. No offence to the latter. But Mr. Valentino was in a category of his own."

"So, Mr. Valentino kept a padlocked cabinet," Ginger started, "Was that his only means of protecting sensitive works?"

"No," Endicott said softly. "There was also a

leather portfolio. It held sketches, letters, rough studies—some very p-private. Correspondence. I saw him with it yesterday, just before we left London."

"And have you seen it since?"

Endicott shook his head. "It's v-vanished. Either he hid it—or someone took it."

"Could it contain motives?" Basil asked.

"Of half the people in this house, if it's what I suspect. Lucien collected s-sins the way some collect stamps."

"One last question," Basil said, tapping his finger on the desktop. "Did Valentino mention any specific threats? Any sense that someone wanted to silence him?"

Endicott paused. "He said this exhibition would be his 'cleansing fire.' That the truth would out. I thought it was a m-metaphor. With Mr. Valentino, you never knew. Performance and p-provocation were his stock-in-trade."

Basil ducked his chin. "Thank you, Endicott. That will be all for now."

He stood, smoothing his jacket. At the door, he paused and glanced back over his shoulder.

"I liked Lucien," he said, almost too softly to hear. "Even when I h-hated him."

Then he stepped out into the corridor, and the door latched shut behind him.

THE STORM HAD EASED—BUT only in volume, not in spirit. The rain now fell in sleeting diagonal threads, needling the skin, and the wind had taken on a mean, swirling edge, kicking gravel into the hems of Ginger's cloak as she and Basil crossed the courtyard behind the manor. The path to the outbuildings, once a tidy stretch of crushed stone, was now a slick, glistening smear underfoot, the puddles brimming with distorted reflections of torchlight from the house.

Behind them, the manor loomed like a half-drowned relic, its lower windows aglow with wavering candlelight. Inside, Boss remained on duty in the drawing room, stationed beside Charles and Felicia. Ginger smiled at the mental image of her little pet, his ears pricked, his stance alert as he guarded the gathered suspects with quiet vigilance.

"I still think we should've waited until morning," Basil half-shouted over the wind.

Ginger tightened her grip on Basil's arm as another gust tugged violently at her hood. "And if we had," she replied, lifting her skirts above the clinging mud, "whatever Endicott hid out here would be long gone by then."

They came upon the coach house, hunched and brooding beneath a sodden shroud of ivy and shadow. The building was older than the main hall by at least a generation—its thick stone walls streaked dark with rain, the wooden shutters bowed and swollen from years of damp. A single lantern dangled above the gable, its flame reduced to a jaundiced flicker, casting more shadow than light.

Basil gave the heavy double doors a once-over. "Hard to tell if this place is meant for horses or ghosts."

Ginger rapped firmly on the wood. The knock echoed with a hollow, almost subterranean timbre.

"No one here," Basil said, bending to peer through a warped pane of glass.

Ginger reached for the handle—solid, iron, and bolted shut. "Locked."

Basil produced a ring of borrowed keys, their brass edges dulled with age. He chose one as if by instinct, and it slid into the lock with a reluctant click.

"Let's see what our meticulous cataloguer was hiding," he murmured.

The door groaned open on protesting hinges, spilling them into musty gloom.

Inside, the air was damp and earthy, laced with the scent of rotting wood, old leather, and rusted metal. Cobwebs shivered in the rafters. A disused carriage rested beneath a dusty tarp. Hooks of tarnished tack lined the walls, and lengths of rotted rope near a barrel of discarded nails.

A single oil lamp was paired with a box of matches. Basil lit the lamp—its flame feeble but steady, casting a cone of gold over a cluttered workbench. Nearby, a few rough crates had been shoved against the walls in a haphazard manner, as though someone had been searching for something—or hiding it.

"There," Ginger said suddenly, pointing towards the rear.

In the far corner, a flat, brown-paper-wrapped package stood propped against an overturned stool. The paper had wicked up moisture from the floor, creating a waterline. Ginger crossed the space cautiously, skirts brushing the puddle-covered stone floor. Basil followed, and they lifted the parcel, undid the string, and carefully folded back the damp brown paper.

Framed under glass was a pastel figure study. Nude. Delicate.

"It bears a striking resemblance to Vivienne Brousseau," Basil said. "Explains why she was invited, though she was the only one besides us without a likeness on auction."

"No," Ginger said, "that's not true. I came across a sketch during the auction that wasn't on display. It quite upset Mlle Brousseau. In fact, I think it might have been a preliminary sketch for this piece."

"This wasn't meant to be seen," Basil said, glancing around. "At least not yet."

"Or someone didn't want it seen at all."

Ginger nodded. "Endicott said Lucien kept a series—sketches, studies, even letters."

She glanced at a nearby crate, the lid half-ajar. Inside were pages—some drawings, others hand-written, some affixed hastily to heavier stock. One appeared to be a piece of writing paper, the image at the top of the page partially obscured by a smudge of charcoal, but recognisable as a family crest. A rampant stag, a broken spear, and beneath it, a barely legible name: Zouch-Nettleby.

Ginger's brows knitted, but she said nothing immediately.

"Is that—?" Basil began.

"Just the Zouch-Nettleby crest."

Basil sifted through the remaining contents— fragments of parchment, half-rendered faces, and scraps of correspondence with initials, most unsigned.

"Lucien was assembling something," Ginger said.

"Endicott didn't just hide this," Basil added. "He quarantined it."

Ginger closed the crate and stood. "Which makes you wonder—was he trying to protect Lucien's legacy... or himself?"

Outside, thunder rumbled in the distance, softer now but insistent, as if the night were warning them not to dig too deep.

Ginger turned towards the door. "We should get back. Before everyone notices we've gone."

CHAPTER THIRTEEN

The tiled floors of the service wing had been scrubbed to a dull, respectable sheen, their black-and-white squares worn smooth in places where decades of boots had passed. The walls bore the faint gloss of whitewash, lined with orderly rows of pegs from which hung a variety of garments: dark wool coats, stout aprons stiff with laundering, and one sturdy oilskin smelling faintly of linseed and salt. The air carried a mingled scent of beeswax polish, banked coal dust from the range, and the comforting aroma of fresh bread cooling on a wire rack—a domestic warmth that sat faintly at odds with the sombre purpose of the visit. Somewhere beyond the scullery door, a clock ticked in time with the slow drip of rain from the eaves.

For a country estate, even a modest one, the staff was strikingly small—something Ginger had noted upon their arrival and now saw plainly as the four assembled in the warm, close kitchen.

Jones stood beside Mrs. Pell whilst Alfred and Betty were in line behind them.

Basil glanced at Ginger before beginning, his voice even. "We'll speak with each of you in turn, but you may remain together unless you'd prefer otherwise."

Jones cleared his throat softly, the sound as discreet as the man himself. "We've nothing to hide, sir."

Ginger offered him a smile she hoped was reassuring. "Perhaps we'll start with you, Jones. I understand you've been with Lady Horatia the longest?"

"Twelve years, madam," he replied, his tone low and precise. "I came to Nettleford Hall after service in the Duke of Axminster's household. Her ladyship required a steady hand after her late husband passed."

"And the staff has remained small since?" Basil asked.

Jones inclined his head almost imperceptibly. "Her ladyship prefers it so. After the war, good help was scarce, and she found she could manage with fewer hands. Fewer people means fewer tongues wagging." His face did not change, but Ginger caught the nuance: Lady Horatia valued discretion above all other virtues.

"Did you know Mr. Lucien Vale?" Ginger asked.

"I knew of him. He has visited here in the past, though not often. An… intense man. I saw more of him during Lady Horatia's London seasons. He and her ladyship have known each other many years."

"Where were you last night, specifically when the lights went off?" Basil asked.

"I was at my post in the front hall," Jones said. "It was my duty to attend the door and keep watch for late arrivals or unexpected callers."

Ginger turned to Mrs. Pell, who had been listening with folded arms and the air of a woman who would not be hurried. "And you, Mrs. Pell—how long have you been here?"

"Six years, madam. Came when the last cook left to marry a greengrocer in town. I keep the kitchen running, see to the linens, make sure the rooms are ready when guests come." Her eyes softened briefly, then sharpened again. "And I do the marketing in the village, which means I hear what's said."

"Could you identify all the guests by sight who are currently on the grounds?" Ginger asked.

Mrs. Pell gave a wry snort. "Most of 'em, or at least knew their names from the talk in the servants' hall. Mr. Valentino, of course—hard to miss, with that voice like he's always addressing a crowd. Can't say I liked him. Too quick with a jest at someone else's expense."

Betty shifted on the settle, her eyes darting toward Mrs. Pell before she looked at Ginger. Ginger's tone gentled. "You were serving in the drawing room, I believe?"

"Yes, madam." The girl's voice was soft, her words halting. "I kept the glasses filled and the plates tidy. I saw Mr. Vale, same as Mrs. Pell said, and Lady Horatia too. I didn't hear what they spoke about, but —" She hesitated, twisting her apron into a tight cord.

"Go on," Ginger encouraged.

"They didn't look pleased, either of 'em. Like they were trying not to be overheard."

Basil exchanged a glance with Ginger before making a note. "And Alfred?"

The footman straightened from the wall. "I was stationed near the stairs, sir. Kept watch on the comings and goings.

"Did you notice anything unusual before..." Ginger let the sentence trail delicately.

The footman's eyes narrowed in thought. "Only that some folks kept disappearing from the drawing room. You expect a bit of wandering about at these affairs, but there was a restlessness in the air. Mr. Valentino spoke with her ladyship alone for a time. No one else went in until they were done."

Ginger let a moment of silence pass, the faint hiss and crackle of the range filling the space. The heat pressed softly at her back, and she caught the yeasty scent of the bread cooling behind her.

"One last question for all of you," she said at last. "Why do you think Lady Horatia keeps her staff so small—truly?"

Jones answered for them, his voice a shade lower. "Privacy, Mrs. Reed. This is an old house, and her ladyship is an old hand at keeping her affairs her own. Too many staff, and you've too many stories walking out the back door."

Mrs. Pell added, with a firm nod, "And we're loyal, as good servants ought to be. She doesn't need more."

"That will be all for now," Basil said. "Thank you for your candour."

As Ginger and Basil stepped back into the draughty service corridor, the warm kitchen air giving way to the cooler breath of the main house,

Ginger lowered her voice. "A loyal staff in a house this size can hide as much as it reveals."

Basil's look was thoughtful. "And it seems Vale's visit was more complicated than polite society might guess."

They walked on, the soft echo of their steps mingling with the muffled tick of a distant clock. Overhead, a floorboard creaked, and somewhere in the depths of the house, a door closed quietly.

CHAPTER FOURTEEN

*B*asil let out a long breath and leaned back in the study desk chair, arms crossed, brow furrowed beneath the weight of too many tangled threads. "I wouldn't mind a short break. Perhaps a fresh cup of tea. Or something stronger."

Ginger gave a faint smile as she stood. "I need to powder my nose."

Truthfully, she needed more than a mirror and a moment of solitude. The case was thick with misdirection, knotted with old secrets and private shames. They were spinning in circles around truths half-hidden and half-remembered. And like everyone else still confined within the draughty bones of Nettleby House, she was beginning to feel the drag of weariness in her limbs and the dullness at the edge of her senses. They couldn't afford to falter now. Not with a killer still among them. Whoever had struck once might strike again.

She crossed the corridor alone, heels muffled on the worn rug, candlelight flickering along the wood-panelled walls. A fresh gust rattled the windows in their casings. She imagined that somewhere in the house, Boss let out a low, warning growl—still posted dutifully in the drawing room, guarding the guests with all the solemnity of a royal sentinel.

Ginger slipped into the powder room.

Soft candlelight glowed from sconces shaped like rosebuds, their petals delicately tinted. The air was gently perfumed with lavender soap, the talcum hush of powder, and the faint chemical tang of old perfume. Everything was clean, tastefully arranged, and somehow suffocating.

Felicia was there. She stood at the mirror, her silhouette motionless but for the careful press of a powder puff to each cheek. The motion was practiced, poised. But hollow.

It was the reflection that betrayed her: a tremor in her hand, the tightness at the corners of her mouth, and eyes too bright with suppressed emotion.

Ginger stepped forward gently. "Darling, you don't have to pretend with me."

Felicia lowered the puff and offered a cool smile. "I'm not pretending," she said. Then, after a beat, "Well. Not very well, apparently."

Ginger joined her at the mirror, adjusting a hairpin that didn't need adjusting. "You've held yourself together admirably. But I imagine seeing that painting must've been a shock."

"A shock?" Felicia's voice broke on a dry laugh. "It was an ambush. An artistic mugging, really." She looked down, gripping the rim of the porcelain basin. "He promised he'd never show it. It was painted years ago. Before Charles. Before I was even properly myself."

The door opened behind them.

Vivienne Brousseau entered, a vision of restraint and fine tailoring. She murmured an apology, gliding to the far sink with practiced grace. Her gown was a column of pearl silk trimmed in jet beading, and her hair was swept into a chignon so precise it looked carved.

Ginger watched her in the mirror, then turned to Felicia and gave her hand a brief, silent squeeze before speaking.

"Mademoiselle Brousseau," Ginger said lightly. "May I ask—how did you know Lucien Valentino?"

Mlle Brousseau met her gaze in the glass. "Through the gallery circuit, Mrs. Reed. I am a collector as well as a dealer. We met first een Paris, then again een New York. He admired my taste. I admired his ruthlessness."

"Ah," Ginger said with a soft smile. "A mutual appreciation of flair."

Mlle Brousseau dabbed at her lips with a tissue, folded it once, and dropped it into the bin. "We understood each other's ambitions. That eez rare, even een the art world."

"And when did you receive your invitation for this evening?" Ginger asked, watching her closely.

"Five days ago," Vivienne replied without hesitation. "Delivered by courier. No return address, but zee envelope was heavy stock—cream, of course— with a note een Lucien's hand. 'A night of reckoning and delight. I trust you will attend.'" She gave a Gallic shrug. "Dramatic. Entirely Lucien."

"You weren't surprised to be invited?"

Mlle Brousseau snapped her compact shut and met Ginger's gaze evenly. "Surprised? Oui. But not reluctant. Lucien had a way of drawing one een— even when one knew better."

The moment stretched. Ginger offered a polite nod, and Mlle Brousseau turned to go.

After the door closed behind her, Ginger reached gently for Felicia's hand and drew her towards the alcove near the chaise longue, lowering her voice. "Is there anything you wanted to say before we were interrupted?"

Felicia hesitated, then gave a small nod. "I'm all right now. I just..." Her gaze flicked toward the closed door. "Lucien and I—it wasn't an affair, if that's what you're wondering. But it wasn't entirely innocent, either. I was reckless. Tired of being the debutante everyone measured by lineage and dowry —not that I had any dowry, but most didn't know that."

Ginger listened without interrupting.

"I asked Lucien not to exhibit the painting," Felicia continued, voice soft. "Begged him, actually. It wasn't just about what it showed—it was what it meant. He captured a version of me I barely recognise anymore. Raw. Unguarded. Desperate to be seen. And now it's been shown in full view, like some cruel souvenir."

Ginger touched her arm. "Charles married you for the woman you are—not the girl you used to be. He knows your history, and he loves you through it."

Felicia gave a watery laugh and shook her head. "It's not just about love, is it? It's about reputation. What it means for him to be tied to me. What people will say?"

"They'll say what they always say," Ginger replied calmly. "Then they'll forget it the moment the next scandal comes along."

Felicia breathed out slowly. "Yes. I hope you're right."

The door swung open again, and Mlle Brousseau reappeared. She paused slightly when she saw them still there. Her expression flickered—surprise? Suspicion?—but was quickly smoothed into polite composure.

"*Mesdames*," she said with a cool nod.

"I'm going to find Charles," Felicia said softly, lifting her chin and straightening her shoulders. The mask of strength was back in place, but Ginger could see the faint shimmer in her eyes. "We have business to attend to."

Vivienne stepped aside with a clipped, "*Pardon.*"

As Felicia disappeared down the corridor, Ginger lingered a moment.

She turned to the Frenchwoman. "If you wouldn't mind—my husband would like a quiet word with you."

Mlle Brousseau hesitated. Just for a beat. Then smiled with polished ease. "Of course."

As Ginger led her down the corridor, her thoughts sharpened. Felicia's secrets were painful, yes—but known. Mlle Brousseau's, on the other hand, shimmered just out of reach. And the way her voice had shifted ever so slightly when she spoke of Lucien's invitation—measured, rehearsed, as if she'd said it before—had not gone unnoticed.

CHAPTER FIFTEEN

The air in the study smelled of aged leather, smoke, and the faint trace of jasmine that preceded Mlle Brousseau as Ginger led her in. The Frenchwoman moved without sound, her heels cushioned by the thick carpet, her presence cloaked in poise and perfume—jasmine, yes, but laced with something darker.

Basil rose from his chair, nodding politely. "Mademoiselle," he said, gesturing to the armchair opposite his own. "Thank you for joining us."

Vivienne Brousseau inclined her head with that trademark serenity. She crossed the room with the liquid grace of a woman accustomed to being watched. When she settled into the chair, it was with the ease of someone who never felt out of place—

her silk skirts arranged just so, one gloved hand smoothing the folds, the other resting delicately on the carved armrest. Her ankles crossed neatly, her smile cool, controlled. It stopped just shy of her eyes.

"We appreciate your time," Basil said, resuming his seat.

Mlle Brousseau offered a polite nod. "Naturally. Though I doubt I can offer anything... startling. Lucien was never dull, but his habits were hardly mysterious."

"We found a pastel drawing, Mademoiselle. Of you."

Mlle Brousseau didn't flinch, but her lashes dipped for the briefest moment. "Lucien drew many women."

"But none were obviously done from a sketch that disturbed you when you found it earlier, Mademoiselle. And furthermore, none of the others were hidden away in the coach house—delivered there privately by Mr. Endicott."

There was a pause—just long enough to register.

Mlle Brousseau turned her gaze towards the fire. "So," she murmured, "he did not burn eet after all."

"No," Basil said. "He kept it. And chose not to exhibit it. Which leaves us wondering—why did he spare you, when all the others were targeted publicly?"

Mlle Brousseau sat still, her shoulders perfectly straight beneath the smooth line of her bodice. Then she turned her face back to them. The mask of composure did not slip, but something behind her eyes cooled.

"Lucien and I were once lovers," she said, her voice low. "Years ago. Montmartre. He was brilliant, savage, intoxicating. I was young and arrogant and convinced that brilliance would never burn me."

She smiled faintly, without warmth. "I was wrong. He painted me because he could. That sketch —eet was not a tribute. It was a tether. Proof of his possession."

"Yet you let him draw it?" Basil asked.

"I did not let him," she replied. "I asked him not to. But Lucien didn't respond to requests. He responded to power. His, never yours."

Ginger's voice softened. "So what happened this time?"

Mlle Brousseau hesitated, her gloved fingers tightening slightly in her lap. Then she exhaled, sharp and controlled. "He sent an invitation. And a message. He planned to display zee sketch. Unless I gave him something een return."

Basil's brows drew together. "What sort of something?"

Mlle Brousseau looked directly at him, unblinking. "A night. One night. With me. He said he wanted to relive what we had. One last time. He promised that if I agreed, he would keep the sketch out of the exhibition."

Ginger's brows lifted slightly. "And you agreed?"

Mlle Brousseau dipped her chin. "I did. I told myself it was a bargain. A transaction. My consent was cold, calculated and strategic." She gave a humourless smile. "But Lucien never allowed anyone to feel een control. That was the real game. Power was not shared. It was extracted."

"When did it happen?" Basil asked.

"Last night. Upstairs at this manor. Lady Horatia understood that Lucien, Endicott and I would be arriving early. Her housekeeper showed us all to our own rooms. He came to mine. We drank absinthe, argued about what art was. Then he kissed me like it was 1922 and he had something to prove." She looked away. "He returned to his room before dawn. Took a package of my cigarettes."

"But it wasn't over," Ginger said quietly.

"Apparently not," Vivienne admitted. "He

promised to destroy it." She added bitterly, "But Lucien broke promises all zee time."

"Do you believe he was going to break his promise of just one night?" Ginger asked.

Vivienne's eyes turned distant. "I do not know. Last night was never about lust. It was leverage. His way of saying, 'I still own you. I can still command you.'" She gave a hollow laugh. "He wanted to see how far I would go to keep my dignity intact."

"Did you think he'd reveal the sketch anyway?" Ginger asked.

"Probably. Eventually. He could not resist zee theatre of it. He would have waited until I was vulnerable. Or triumphant. And then he would unveil it with a flourish and a toast."

Basil's tone was low. "So you had motive. Coercion. Humiliation. Revenge."

Mlle Brousseau lifted her chin. "Oui, I suppose I did. But so did half zee guest list." She stood, smoothing her skirt with long, deliberate strokes. She walked towards the door but stopped short of touching the knob.

"If I had killed him," she said calmly, "I would have done it een Paris. Neatly. Quietly. And not while stuck een a draughty English country house with a crowd of champagne-soaked witnesses and a couple of amateur sleuths."

Ginger and Basil shared a look of amusement at this obvious slight.

Mlle Brousseau turned, her profile catching the low firelight. "Lucien used to say I was too polished to be dangerous. But polish eez just armour. And armour, *mes cheris*" she smiled thinly, "—eez made for war."

CHAPTER SIXTEEN

A knock sounded—twice, deliberate—before the study door opened again.

"Lady Partridge, sir, madam," Alfred announced, stifling a yawn behind his gloved hand.

Lady Ione Partridge entered with her head high, shoulders square, and her peacock-feathered head-piece bobbing precariously with each purposeful step. The heavy folds of her embroidered shawl draped dramatically from her shoulders, trailing behind her. One bejewelled hand clutched a silver-handled cane, clearly ornamental.

Her perfume arrived before her—a bold, nostalgic cloud of something musky, floral, and faintly powdery, the scent of a dowager's vanity layered over a dancer's dressing room. The effect was as unforgettable as it was invasive.

"My dears," she trilled, halting in the centre of the rug and striking a pose. "I do hope I'm not your next suspect. Though I suppose it's only fair—scandal and I have long been acquainted."

"Lady Partridge," Ginger said, gesturing with an open hand towards the vacant armchair. "Thank you for joining us."

"Oh, I wouldn't miss it for the world," she declared. "The scandal tonight is positively intoxicating."

Ginger raised a brow. "A man is dead."

"Oh yes, I know," Lady Partridge said with a wave of her hand. "May he rest in peace."

With a flourish of her shawl and a loud sigh of noble inconvenience, she lowered herself into the chair, the process resembling a grand descent from an opera box. Once seated, she tugged her hem just so, fanned the edge of her shawl with deliberate fingers, and adjusted a rather large emerald ring on her index finger as if to catch the firelight.

"I hope you don't mind a few questions," Basil said.

"Mind?" she echoed with a throaty laugh that morphed into a genteel cough. "Darling, it's the most excitement I've had since that regrettable incident with the Turkish ambassador's monkey in '22."

Ginger was surprised. "You seemed rather upset on seeing Mr. Valentino's body."

"I was shocked, Mrs. Reed. Despite my reputation for adventure, the only dead bodies I've ever seen before tonight were well-made up corpses in open coffins. I just couldn't believe what my eyes were seeing. Blood hasn't pumped through my heart quite like that in a very long time."

Basil smiled politely. "I'd like to begin by asking you about the painting Lucien Valentino displayed tonight. 'Widow's Mantle'."

Lady Partridge lifted her chin with a dignified sniff. "Yes, well. A ghastly little thing, wasn't it? All metaphor and innuendo. Again."

"Again?"

"Oh yes. This was the second version he painted of it, brought up to date. The last one was painted when I was still married to my second husband."

"You claimed to adore it," Basil noted.

She straightened her shawl and gave a theatrical shrug. "What choice did I have? He unveiled it at a charity gala, society reporters standing by with sharpened pencils. I couldn't very well scream and throw my drink—not in front of the Duchess of

Marlborough. Though I was sorely tempted. So I was left with no option but to claim admiration and to buy the thing."

"But it never appeared in your home," Ginger said. "I heard it mentioned you claimed it was lost in shipping."

Lady Partridge leaned forward, her rings glittering in the candle light. "And what would you have preferred I say? That I wrapped it in oilcloth and buried it beneath the stables? I'm vain, not deranged. I don't keep my own defamation above the piano."

"Did you know Valentino had painted another version and intended to display it again tonight?" Basil asked.

"I suspected," she replied with a bitter little smile. "Lucien had a flair for the vindictive. He never let a brushstroke go to waste if it could still draw blood."

"Did you confront him?"

She leaned back with an exaggerated flutter of her shawl and one raised eyebrow. "Good heavens, no. I smiled, I drank something bubbly, and I pretended to be delighted—just as one does when an old lover appears across the ballroom with a new waistline. One feigns amnesia."

"Lady Partridge," Ginger started, "was there

anyone at this gathering Mr. Valentino might have hesitated to offend?"

A low chuckle rasped from her throat. "Lucien? My dear, he offended for sport. He once insulted a Spanish ambassador and a duchess in a single sketch and sold it to the German Embassy. But if I were the cautious type—and I'm not—I wouldn't have crossed Lady Horatia."

"Socially?" Basil asked.

"Oh no," she said, eyes glittering. "Professionally. During the war, Lady Horatia wasn't just clipping roses and composing poetry for wounded officers. She worked in a discreet branch of the Foreign Office. As did Dorian March. Censorship, propaganda, and what they so delicately called 'art recovery.'"

"Recovery?" Ginger echoed.

"That's the polite term." Lady Partridge leaned forward, lowering her voice to a stage whisper. "She helped coordinate the removal of stolen artworks from occupied territories. That's what the record says, anyway. But there were whispers—paintings meant for safe return that never found their way home. Masterworks declared destroyed, only to turn up in the sitting rooms of certain peers or locked away in private estates."

Her voice dropped further. "Lady Horatia's house in Paris has one of the finest post-Impressionist collections outside Paris. That didn't fall into her lap by accident."

Basil frowned. "You're suggesting she kept the art."

"I'm not suggesting anything," Lady Partridge replied sweetly. "I'm simply saying she knows more about art theft than most women of her generation. And she's better at keeping it quiet."

"How did you come by this information?" Ginger asked.

"Oh, my dears, it's the worst-kept secret in certain drawing rooms. I've never seen a forged provenance myself, but I've heard whispers in Paris and Vienna—and from a particularly chatty countess in Aix-en-Provence who claimed to recognise a missing Degas over Horatio's breakfast table."

"Did Lucien know?" Basil asked.

She smirked. "He hinted. Called her the Gorgon of Grosvenor Street. Said she kept secrets in frames. I thought it was all just artistic venom. But after tonight?" She gave a delicate shrug. "I wonder."

Basil exchanged a glance with Ginger.

"Thank you, Lady Partridge," Ginger said. "That will be all for now."

Lady Partridge stood with unexpected grace. She gathered her shawl, adjusted her headpiece with a practiced twist of two fingers, and turned to the door. Just before exiting, she paused and looked over one shoulder.

"If I'm murdered next," she said airily, "do make sure the police photograph me with good lighting."

And with that, she swept out.

Basil exhaled. "Well. That was… theatrical."

"She buried the knife in three layers of lace," Ginger murmured, "but she may have just cracked the case wide open."

Basil nodded. "It's time we had a word with Lady Horatia."

CHAPTER SEVENTEEN

*T*he voices reached them before they got to the drawing room doors.

Raised. Overlapping. Heated.

The clink of glass. A chair scraping across the floor.

And then—

"Oh, do sit down, Nathaniel, you're not in your counting house now!" Delphine Valentino's voice, sharp as crystal.

"You insufferable—" Mr. Zane's growl, bitten off in frustration.

"That's quite enough," came Charles's baritone, strained but commanding.

Ginger and Basil exchanged a look before pushing through the double doors.

The room was a portrait of unraveling elegance. Guests drooped like wilting bouquets—limbs draped, jackets unbuttoned, faces drawn and rumpled, keeping as far from one another as the room would allow. Masks lay abandoned on cushions. The glamour of the evening had come apart at the seams.

Boss padded over to Ginger, head low, tail stiff, ears pricked. He let out a soft, uneasy grumble.

"It's nearly three o'clock," Lady Partridge muttered, hiding a genteel yawn behind her hand. "I'm in danger of embarrassing myself by falling asleep in public."

"You mean snoring," Mlle Brousseau said, with a pointed glance. The Frenchwoman was beginning to look haggard with fatigue. "Are not we all? Lady Horatia, surely even prisoners get beds."

"I've already offered, darling," Lady Horatia said coolly. "But our dear Chief Inspector and his charming wife insist we remain under observation."

"Ah," Mlle Brousseau said ironically. "I assume answering a call of nature eez still permitted?"

Basil gave a curt nod.

"I'll come too," Nola Plimpton said quickly, already moving to the door, her eye cast downward.

As they exited, Lady Horatia's voice rang out. "I

think we could all use more coffee. Where is Betty? She's probably fast asleep in some corner." She turned to Endicott. "Endicott, go see what's become of the maid, will you?"

Endicott looked relieved to be given a task. "Y-yes, Lady Horatia." He deposited his glass and slipped out.

Felicia caught Ginger's eye. "We tried to keep everyone calm," she murmured. "But nerves are fraying."

Mr. Zane rounded again on Miss Valentino, voice rising. "I've never forgiven him. Or you."

Miss Valentino took a slow sip. "Lucien painted what he saw. And what he saw was a predator draped in patronage."

"You have no blasted idea what he saw," Mr. Zane snapped. "You just assumed, like always."

"Oh, let them carry on," Lady Partridge said. "More fun than the wireless. Honestly, who knew Miss Valentino had such bite?"

"Miss Valentino implied she had history with Zane," Basil murmured to Ginger. "Lovers?"

Ginger nodded. "Clearly."

Miss Valentino let out a sharp breath and turned on her heel. "Excuse me," she said icily. "I too, must visit the loo." She swept out, leaving her half-finished drink sweating on the trolley.

Mlle Brousseau returned without Miss Plimpton, passing Miss Valentino as she left. "This eez madness," she said flatly. "We are being rounded up like suspects while zee killer—whoever it ees—ees likely watching us unravel."

"You sound defensive," Lady Horatia said sweetly. "Struck a nerve, darling?"

"Unlike you," Mlle Brousseau replied, "I do not need to perform."

"What ho, Mademoiselle, I think you do," Mr. Zane cut in. "You've been performing all evening. For Lucien, and now for everyone else."

Lady Horatia took a measured sip of tea and glanced towards the door as Betty demurely stepped in. "Coffee and cake," she repeated with an arch of one brow. "And perhaps a cool drink for Lady Partridge. She's beginning to wilt."

"I'm perfectly upright," Lady Partridge huffed. "Unlike certain reputations in this room."

Miss Plimpton returned looking wan and more shaken than ever and dropped heavily into the nearest empty chair.

"Is no one sorting the refreshments?" Lady Partridge asked. "If one wants something done properly—"

"I fetched the maid," Endicott said as he stepped into the room. "She'll return with something soon."

Mr. Zane tapped his cigarette case. "Where's March?" he asked, brow furrowing. "Slipped out for a smoke, I expect. Not a bad idea." He strolled towards the side doors. "Pip pip!"

"I could use air myself," Mlle Brousseau said, stretching. She covered a yawn with the back of her hand. "The veranda, perhaps? Unless men have exclusive rights to oxygen tonight."

"That wind will ruin your hair," Lady Horatia admonished.

Mlle Brousseau tapped the base of her bob. "That is the beauty of short hair. *Très libérateur.*

Charles raised a hand. "Let's keep it orderly. No one alone, please. And stay in view." To Ginger and Basil, he added, "I think I should go too, find out what March is up to."

"Good idea," Ginger said. "And Felicia, love, perhaps you could check on Miss Valentino. She's been in the ladies for a while now."

"Lady Horatia," Basil started. "It was actually you we wanted to speak with."

"I was wondering when you'd come for me. Shall

we go to the study or remain here, since we're alone now?"

Ginger glanced at Endicott positioned by a far window. Clearly he counted as staff in Lady Horatia's eyes and was therefore invisible.

"Someone could return at any time and disturb us," Basil said. "Let's step into the study for privacy sake."

Lady Horatia gave a slight nod. "Very well."

Ginger paused just outside the study door, which stood half- ajar. Boss trotted ahead his hackles up. To Basil she said, "We left this door closed."

Basil pushed it open further.

The fire had burned low, casting long shadows across the carpet and the polished wood of the writing desk. One of the armchairs was tipped over and lying on its side, but that wasn't what caught the eye.

Dorian March was slumped over the desk, one arm outstretched as though reaching for something, the other curled beneath him. His cheek was pressed awkwardly to the wood. Beneath his face, a fan of papers had scattered, some of them spattered with crimson.

The handle of a brass letter opener jutted grotesquely from his back.

Basil sprang to the door and pushed Lady Horatia back out into the passage before she could see.

"One moment, Lady Horatia. Please go back to the drawing room, we will fetch you again shortly."

He stepped back into the study and closed the door in Lady Horatia's face. Ginger stepped forward quickly but carefully, eyes flicking over the scene. Boss stayed by the threshold, letting out a low, uncertain growl.

Basil reached the desk first, fingers gently brushing Mr. March's wrist. "No pulse," he said grimly. "Of course not."

Ginger circled to Mr. March's other side, kneeling slightly to examine the angle of the blade. "Thrust from behind. No wild struggle—he likely never even stood up."

She touched the blotting paper beside him—it was still damp with ink. The teacup had overturned as he collapsed, soaking the papers near the edge. A spoon rested a few inches away, its bowl bent ever so slightly, as though clutched in a final movement.

"Who could've done this?" Ginger said.

Basil stroked his chin. "Everyone was together in the drawing room at one point."

"Then, Vivienne Brousseau and Nola Plimpton left for the toilets."

"Lady Horatia sent Endicott on an errand."

"Delphine Valentino leaves, as Mlle Brousseau returns," Ginger added, "Followed by Miss Plimpton, then Endicott."

"Miss Valentino remains unaccounted for," Basil said, "hopefully to be found shortly by Felicia."

"Don't forget that Mr. Zane left to have a cigarette," Ginger said, stretching out her arms and relieving a kink in her neck. "Mlle Brousseau was eager to follow."

Basil raised a brow. "Do you think they worked together to kill March?"

"I haven't the faintest idea," Ginger admitted. "there was so much coming and going, I'm dizzy thinking about it."

Basil frowned. "Indeed. It's a shame we weren't more careful."

CHAPTER EIGHTEEN

*H*alf an hour later, Lady Horatia followed Ginger and Basil, this time into the library, Charles and the footman were moving the body of Mr. March into the cold room. The wood-panelled library was lined with towering shelves of leather-bound volumes, their spines gleaming in the firelight. Deep chairs and the scent of old paper and polished oak produced an air of both refinement and secrecy.

Lady Horatia crossed to the tall windows, pushed aside the brocade curtain, and rested one hand on the sill, studying her reflection in the glass against the darkness outside. In her other hand, a cigarette smouldered low between two bejewelled fingers.

Her mask had been discarded, but not the performance.

She turned slowly, her expression composed, her smile measured. "Mrs. Reed. Chief Inspector. What a spectacular turn of events. Honestly, I assumed Lucien had taken his own life, drunkenly hugging his beloved statue. But now..."

Ginger tilted her head. "What led you to believe Mr. Valentino would do such a thing? And on a night like this?"

Lady Horatia gave a dry little laugh. "Lucien was the embodiment of drama and unpredictability, darling. He lived to astonish people—he loved nothing more than shocking a room into silence. Add to that his fondness for certain opiates, and it's hardly a stretch. He was insensible half the time. The other half, he thought himself immortal. I wouldn't be the least surprised if he genuinely believed he might rise from the dead."

She sauntered across the room and lowered herself into the nearest armchair with feline grace. Crossing her ankles, she rested her cigarette hand lightly on the armrest and exhaled a fine plume of smoke.

"He had," she added with a sigh, "what one might call a God complex."

"You knew Dorian March from your Foreign Office days," Basil said pointedly.

Lady Horatia arched a thin, carefully maintained brow. "My darling Chief Inspector, I've never publicly admitted to having worked in such a place. I chaired aid committees. Organised comforts for convalescing officers. That's all anyone needs to know."

"But in truth?" Basil prompted.

"In truth," she said, her voice cooling, "Dorian and I were part of a rather more... discreet wartime initiative. Intelligence and censorship. We handled intercepted communiqués, filtered propaganda, classified transcripts. Dorian had a singular mind for patterns, codes, hidden meanings. He could see the shape of a thing long before it emerged. Which made him brilliant. And dangerous." She narrowed her gaze. "I'm only telling you this because two men have died."

"Dangerous to whom?" Ginger asked.

Lady Horatia flicked ash delicately into the crystal dish beside her. "To the wrong people. One might argue Lucien Valentino was among them. Not during the war—but later. Lucien had a way of sniffing out secrets. Dorian warned me before he left for Austria that Lucien had acquired a copy of something... sensitive. I never learned what it was. Only that it had to do with Vienna, 1917."

Ginger sat forward slightly. "Did you fear Mr. Valentino might reveal something about you?"

"No," Lady Horatia said quickly. Then, with a soft sigh, "Not fear. But I've always believed in the virtue of caution. Lucien collected secrets and used them as currency. And like any man with an inflated sense of power, he thought himself above consequence."

Ginger nodded, letting that sit. "What did you think of his exhibition last night?"

Lady Horatia stubbed out her cigarette and waved a hand. "Grotesque, mostly. The pieces lacked soul. All spectacle, no substance. By the end, he was more impresario than artist. A showman. A provocateur. The art itself became secondary."

"Were you aware he intended to display the painting of Lady Davenport-Witt?"

Lady Horatia's mouth twitched. "Yes. I warned him not to exhibit it—or any of them, honestly. The entire evening was a powder keg dressed in feathers and velvet. I told him it would end badly. He laughed, of course, saying that scandal was the only honest currency left in polite society."

"Do you know who might have wanted Valentino dead?" Basil asked.

Lady Horatia gave a dark little chuckle. "You might do better asking who wouldn't."

"What about Mr. March?" Ginger prompted. "How did he fit into Mr. Valentino's plans for the night? And who would want him dead?"

"Lucien's goal was simple: revenge, dressed as revelation," Lady Horatia said. "He meant to embarrass everyone he once envied—or felt betrayed by. Dorian was an easy target. He was once Lucien's protégé, you know. A long time ago. Like he does with everyone he knows, Lucien used him, manipulated him, and discarded him when he outlived his usefulness. Dorian struck back, years ago, with a devastating critique—an essay under Lucien's name that ruined a gallery's reputation. It was venomously clever."

Ginger's eyes narrowed. "Was that essay truly written by Mr. March?"

"Indeed," Lady Horatia said. "Though few ever knew it. Lucien, naturally, was outraged. Delphine, however, found it all rather amusing."

Ginger and Basil exchanged a glance.

"She did?" Ginger said. "Why?"

Lady Horatia leaned back, lips curling. "Because she paid Dorian to write it."

"She paid Dorian March?" Basil asked, startled.

"Oh yes. A lover's revenge. The gallery owner was a former lover of hers. She wanted him brought low."

"And Mr. March obliged?" Ginger asked.

Lady Horatia shrugged one elegant shoulder. "He liked to play at being principled, but he had a streak of cruelty. And he needed the money. Delphine was clever enough to wrap it all in artistic justification."

Ginger pressed, "Do you know the name of the curator?"

"I do. It was Nathaniel Zane." There was a beat of silence as Lady Horatia stood. "If you don't mind, I'm exhausted. I must go back to my guests, such as are left."

Ginger remained seated for a moment, her gaze fixed on the hearth, where the last embers glowed a soft, dying orange beneath a husk of grey ash. The shadows in the study had grown long. Outside, the wind had stilled, leaving the manor in an eerie hush.

"Well," she said finally, "Lady Horatia was either a font of information or a mistress of misdirection."

"Possibly both," Basil said, folding his arms as he leaned against the edge of the desk. "But we can't dismiss the possibility that she was telling the truth. At least, her version of it."

Ginger tilted her head. "She slipped, though. That

'no' came out too fast when I asked if she feared Lucien Valentino might expose her. And then she softened. Guilt, maybe. Or... regret?"

"Or calculation," Basil offered. "She's a practised hand at managing perception. She knows when to reveal and when to retreat. Did you notice how she framed March? As a gifted mind ruined by vice and betrayal. Simultaneously a victim and a saboteur."

Ginger's brow furrowed. "It's a contradiction."

"Unless," Basil said, "both sides are true."

"Let' not forget how Nathaniel Zane's name slipped in. Everyone here, beside us, are all entangled with each other somehow."

They fell into silence for a beat. The fire snapped and settled, casting long shadows against the panelling.

"What do you make of this claim that Delphine paid March to ruin Zane's gallery?" Basil asked, breaking the quiet. "It's quite the accusation, even from someone as comfortably cynical as Lady Horatia."

Ginger stretched out her legs as she suppressed a yawn. "It wouldn't surprise me. Delphine exuded a kind of amused cruelty last night—watching the evening spiral as if it were a play she'd already seen.

She drifted through the chaos untouched, unbothered. And the way she looked at Zane..."

She stopped, turning slightly toward Basil. "There was smugness there. Like she knew he was dancing on strings he couldn't see."

"It seems the Valentino siblings were alike in that way," Basil said. "They both weaponised secrets. They both delighted in watching the impact from a safe distance."

"We've got a house full of people with reasons to lie," Ginger started, "to lash out, to protect old wounds."

"And two bodies," Basil said. Under his breath, he added, "So far."

Ginger exhaled slowly. "Trying to solve this case is like trying to finish one of those jigsaw puzzles while someone keeps shifting the edge pieces." She gave a tired smile. "And I daresay the picture on the box was a forgery all along."

They stood together in the hush, then Ginger added, "I suppose in light of what's happened, we need to talk to them all again. Who should we start with, Miss Valentino or Mr. Zane?"

Wearily, Basil grinned. "We could toss a coin." He pulled a half-penny from his pocket and flipped it into the air.

CHAPTER NINETEEN

The drawing room had settled into the hush that follows an emotional storm. The air was heavy with fatigue and uncertainty. Guests had slumped into armchairs and settees, the glamour of the previous evening now slouched and faded. The fire crackled listlessly in the grate. A tray of fresh tea had been placed on a sideboard, but few seemed inclined to touch it.

Basil stood and scanned the room, his eyes narrowing. "Where's Mr. Zane?"

Ginger followed Basil's gaze toward the far corner, where Mr. Zane had last been seated near the drinks trolley. The wingback chair sat empty. "He's not here," she said quietly.

Basil's eyes moved swiftly from face to face. "Nor is Miss Valentino."

Ginger turned a slow circle. "Did anyone see where Mr. Zane or Miss Valentino went?"

The other guests stirred, looking about uncertainly, as if only just realising something—or someone—was missing.

"I thought they were still here," Lady Partridge said from her upright perch near the windows, her voice dry as parchment.

"They were here when I returned," Lady Horatia added crisply from her station near the fireplace. "Miss Valentino slipped out first. I assumed she went to the ladies' powder room."

Charles and Felicia joined Ginger and Basil at the edge of the room. Charles looked around with concern. "They were just here."

"I only closed my eyes for a moment," Felicia added, a slight tremble in her voice. "Surely they haven't—"

"We don't know anything yet," Basil said, cutting in gently. "But we need to find them."

Charles squared his shoulders and straightened his jacket. "I'll take the north corridor. Check the gallery and the side parlour."

"I'll come with you," Felicia said. "We'll try

upstairs too, if nothing turns up. At least we know they haven't stepped out in this weather."

The storm outside had turned to sleet, lashing against the windows with wet fury. The wind moaned faintly under the eaves.

As the pair disappeared into the hall, Ginger touched Basil's sleeve and nodded toward a more secluded corner of the room.

"While we wait," she said softly, "we can speak with one of the others."

Lady Ione Partridge sat like a relic in her carved wooden chair, her posture as stiff as the high collar of her gown. Her black jet beads caught the firelight like shards of night. She watched Ginger and Basil approach without the slightest flicker of surprise.

Ginger offered her a tight smile and took the seat opposite. Basil remained standing, angled slightly behind her.

"We're sorry to bother you again, Lady Partridge."

"I can't say I'm surprised. However, even now you won't get sentiment from me," she said briskly, brushing a non-existent speck from her sleeve. "Lucien Valentino was always going to die in a manner of high drama. I simply thought he'd plan it himself."

"So you didn't like him," Basil said.

"As you might have guessed from what I said before, I found him corrosive," she replied flatly. "Entertaining in small doses—at a distance. Up close, the man was intolerable. I came tonight purely out of curiosity. I wanted to see how far he'd push it."

"And how far would that be?" Ginger asked.

Lady Partridge gave a cool, thin smile. "Too far, evidently."

"Do you know who might have had reason to stop him?" Basil asked.

She gave a short, derisive breath. "Pick a name out of a hat. Delphine Valentino? Zane? Half the room? Lucien left a trail of egos in ruins and secrets laid bare. He was like a fox with a taste for feathers— he couldn't resist stirring up the henhouse."

Ginger let a beat pass, then asked, "And Vivienne Brousseau? Would you put her name in that hat?"

Lady Partridge's eyes gleamed with sudden interest as she stared across the room. Her gaze settled on the lady in question—Vivienne Brousseau —who sat near the mantelpiece with her arms folded tightly across her lap, feigning disinterest. But her posture was too rigid, her stare too fixed on nothing at all.

"Ah," Lady Partridge murmured, lips curling.

"The quiet Frenchwoman. I did wonder when she'd come up."

"We're asking about everyone," Basil said evenly.

"Well, she certainly doesn't look pleased to be here," Lady Partridge replied, folding her hands with prim satisfaction. "Always hovering near the edges, watching with those wide, unreadable eyes."

"Did you hear anything between her and Lucien?" Ginger asked.

"No," Lady Partridge said. "But I saw a look that passed between them at the auction. It wasn't embarrassment on her part. It was fury. Controlled, yes—but unmistakable. It's my belief he had something on her. And she knew the clock was running out."

"You believe she had motive, then?" Basil asked.

"I believe," Lady Partridge said coolly, "that Miss Brousseau has carried a very old, very expensive secret for some time. And that Mr. March—clever little viper that he was—found it out."

Ginger leaned in slightly. "What kind of secret?"

Lady Partridge tilted her head. "I'm not in the habit of spreading art world gossip, Mrs. Reed. But since we're all trapped here, and a murderer is amongst us... I suppose it's relevant."

She lowered her voice to a confidential murmur.

"Years ago, Vivienne sold a painting at an international auction—quite a high-profile sale. Only the work wasn't genuine. The provenance documents were forged. A major scandal, had it ever come to light. But it never did."

Ginger's brows lifted. "And Dorian March knew?"

Lady Partridge gave a satisfied nod. "He did. And Lucien knew he knew. In fact, Lucien kept him quiet —perhaps out of loyalty, perhaps because Vivienne was useful to him. But Lucien's protection died with him, didn't it?"

"And Dorian wanted compensation," Basil said grimly.

"Oh, I would imagine, yes," Lady Partridge replied. "Word has it he came to Vivienne not long ago, asking for money. A generous sum, in exchange for silence. Or else."

"Blackmail," Ginger said softly.

"Call it what you like," Lady Partridge said, rising smoothly to her feet. "But a woman cornered is a dangerous thing—especially one with a past like that."

She adjusted the folds of her gown and added, almost idly, "I heard Dorian muttering in French during the gallery showing. Something acidic. Vivienne turned her head like she'd been slapped. Didn't speak a word—but recognition, oh yes. There was history there."

Ginger studied the older woman. "You're remarkably observant, Lady Partridge."

"I've had decades to perfect the art," she replied, brushing invisible lint from her sleeve. "And I've learned one thing with certainty—it's rarely the loud ones who strike. It's the quiet ones. The ones who watch. And wait."

She turned, then glided across the room to the fireplace.

Basil leaned in to Ginger. "That was less an observation than a full prosecution."

"She certainly made it sound like motive," Ginger murmured. "Now let's find out if Mlle Brousseau agrees."

The tension in the drawing room was beginning to coil again. Whispered conversations flickered from one sofa to the next. A glance at the clock on the mantel told Ginger that nearly twenty minutes had passed since Mr. Zane and Miss Valentino had last been seen.

Then the door creaked open.

All heads turned.

Delphine Valentino stepped inside, as poised as if

she'd just come in from a luncheon at Claridge's. Her dress had been adjusted at the waist, and her lipstick reapplied. A few droplets of rain still clung to her shoulder wrap.

"Good heavens," Lady Horatia muttered. "Where have you been?"

Miss Valentino blinked once, then smiled faintly. "Powdering my nose, darling. Though I must say, the facilities are ghastly. Freezing tiles and only a tiny mirror."

"You've been gone ages," Basil said, stepping toward her. "We were concerned."

"Were you?" she asked lightly, pulling off her gloves one finger at a time. "That's very touching. But I assure you, I'm quite fine."

Ginger crossed the room to meet her. "Miss Valentino, forgive the directness, but we were told you left the drawing room just before Mr. Zane did. Neither of you announced your departure, and he has not returned."

Miss Valentino tilted her head. "Nathaniel?" A pause. "I haven't seen him."

"You weren't with him?" Ginger asked.

"Certainly not." The answer came quickly. "Why on earth would I scarper off with Nathaniel Zane?"

"You tell us," Basil said evenly. "You both vanished within minutes of each other."

Miss Valentino's eyes flashed with something—irritation, perhaps, or calculation. "Chief Inspector, I appreciate that your job is to connect dots, but this is hardly a painting. Sometimes two people go missing for entirely separate reasons. If Nathaniel's taken it upon himself to wander off, I suggest you look to him for an explanation."

She swept past them, reclaiming her previous seat near the fire, folding her legs with exaggerated grace.

"Honestly," she added, "all this fuss over men disappearing. You'd think no one ever left a room before. And good Lord. I'm about to fall asleep in this chair. So undignified."

CHAPTER TWENTY

*B*asil stepped to the centre of the drawing room, the light of the oil lamp picking out the silver streaks at his temples.. The room quieted almost at once. Conversations fell away, replaced by the low pop and hiss of the fire.

He cleared his throat and spoke with quiet authority.

"I must ask that no one leave this room," he said, his voice carrying easily across the high-ceilinged chamber. "Not for the corridor, not for the powder room. We will continue our inquiries here. For your safety, and in the interest of truth."

A ripple of murmurs followed—some indignant, others weary, none defiant. A few guests exchanged looks over the rims of teacups. Lady Partridge arched a single eyebrow in theatrical amusement, while Lady Horatia pressed her lips together and looked away.

Ginger touched Basil's sleeve, then gave a slight nod toward the hearth.

Vivienne Brousseau sat apart from the others, perched in a small Queen Anne armchair upholstered in faded blue damask. The glow of the fire lit one side of her face, casting the other in shadow. Her gown—a column of pearl silk trimmed in jet beading—was immaculate, but her posture was not. She was half-turned from the room, as though trying to disappear into the fire's warmth. Her black shawl clung tightly around her shoulders despite the heat.

Her eyes met Ginger's as she approached—dark eyes, sharp and unreadable, now ringed with fatigue.

"Mademoiselle Brousseau," Ginger said gently, pulling a straight-backed chair closer. "Would you mind answering a few more questions?"

Mlle Brousseau's gaze flicked briefly to Basil, then back again. Her nod was slow, composed. "If eet will help," she replied, her accent thicker now, as though weariness were tugging her back across the Channel.

Ginger held her gaze. "We've heard that Dorian March may have been blackmailing you."

Mlle Brousseau's jaw clenched. She turned toward the fire, the light flickering over the sweep of her cheekbone. "You have been speaking with Lady Partridge, I presume?" Her tone carried both disdain and resignation. "She plays a very old game. A sharp tongue wrapped een old lace."

"But the accusation?" Basil prompted.

Mlle Brousseau was silent for a moment. Then, deliberately, she opened her hands.

"There was a painting," she said softly. "Not mine, not truly. Years ago, een Paris, I allowed my name to be used to authenticate a forged provenance. The buyer was powerful. The auction—international. Had zee deception come to light, eet would have ended my career."

"But it didn't," Basil said.

"No, because Lucien... arranged things. He kept Dorian silent, though not for my sake."

"You're saying Lucien used your secret as leverage?" Ginger asked.

Mlle Brousseau gave a single, tight nod. "He protected zee secret only as long as eet served him. Dorian stayed quiet. For a time."

"What changed?" Basil asked.

Mlle Brousseau looked away. "Three weeks ago, Dorian approached me. He said with Lucien's exhibition coming, zee timing was ideal to 'correct zee past.' Of course, he meant payment. He wanted money—for his silence."

"And Lucien?" Ginger asked. "Did he know?"

Mlle Brousseau considered. "I believe so. He made a comment—odd, casual—that I should 'mind what debts I pretend have been forgotten.' He did not mention Dorian by name, but I knew."

Her eyes, usually so still, flared with something more dangerous now—fury, sorrow, or perhaps shame.

"I will not cry for either of them," she said. "But I did not kill them."

She turned her eyes to Basil. "I did not kill them."

Mlle Brousseau rose before they could say more, smoothing her gown with a swift flick of the wrist. "If you are finished…" she said coolly, and without waiting for permission, she crossed the room and lowered herself into a tufted chair beneath a portrait of a dour Victorian gentleman. She stared at her hands, her features unreadable once more.

Ginger exhaled slowly. "That didn't sound like a lie."

"No," Basil said, watching Mlle Brousseau closely. "But it didn't sound like the full truth either."

Ginger's gaze landed on Nola Plimpton. She held

a teacup in both hands, though she hadn't sipped. Steam rose, forgotten. Her mouse-brown hair had mostly slipped its pins, and her silver-embroidered shawl, too gaudy for her, hung limply on her narrow shoulders, the ends wrapped over her wrists as if she were cold.

Ginger nudged Basil. "Perhaps it's time to speak with the quiet one."

"Right-o," Basil said.

Together they turned to the fragile form of the young lady folded into the and of a brocade settee. The fire's glow didn't seem to reach her.

"Miss Plimpton," Ginger began when they reached her.

"Yes?" Miss Plimpton said weakly.

Ginger lowered herself onto the other end of the settee as Basil remained standing. "Are you quite all right, Miss Plimpton?" Ginger asked. "You look rather pale."

"It's all a lot to take in, isn't it, Mrs. Reed?"

"Indeed," Basil answered, "and that's what necessitates that we ask you a few questions."

Miss Plimpton nodded. "Yes. I understand. It's all so… *frightful*."

Her voice edged up so high on the word "frightful," Ginger worried the chandelier might crack.

"You knew Mr. Valentino only in passing?" Basil asked gently, his tone neutral but watchful.

"Yes. I mean—we were at a few functions together. He'd once painted a friend of mine. Not me, of course. I'm not... Was not..." Her voice drifted into silence, and she stared into her teacup.

"Not the type he usually painted?" Ginger prompted, her brow raised slightly.

Nola Plimpton gave a short, breathy laugh that caught on something in her throat. "Oh, well—he liked drama, didn't he? Women with teeth. Scandals. Mystery. I'm afraid I've never been mysterious."

"No one's life is as simple as it appears," Ginger said, her voice softening.

Miss Plimpton glanced up at that, and for a moment something flickered in her eyes—amusement, perhaps, or pain. She twisted the fringe of her shawl between two fingers. "I suppose not."

"You purchased a piece from the auction," Basil said. "Paper Wings."

Miss Plimpton stiffened slightly. "Yes."

"It made quite an impression," Ginger said. "A schoolgirl with wings made of watercolour paintings, teetering on the edge of a burning stage."

"A shadow watching from the wings," Basil added.

Miss Plimpton's teacup clinked against its saucer as her hands trembled. "It was... personal."

"Was the girl you?" Ginger asked gently.

Miss Plimpton hesitated. "Parts of her."

"And the shadow?" Basil asked.

Another long pause.

"Some men like to collect clever girls," Miss Plimpton said at last. "They lift you up just enough to watch you fall. It's not always physical. Sometimes it's worse when it isn't. Lucien knew how to... encourage."

Her voice caught again. "He made promises. About my work. About exhibitions. Then changed the terms once he knew I'd... invested. He said my paintings wouldn't be shown if I didn't play along."

Ginger's gaze sharpened. "Did you?"

Miss Plimpton nodded once, quickly. "One night. It was enough."

She took a trembling breath. "I wanted the paintings out there. I wanted someone to see them. To see me. But," her voice turned bitter, "then he refused to exhibit them."

"And what about Mr. March?" Basil asked after a moment.

The colour drained from Miss Plimpton's face.

She looked down, folding her hands tightly in her lap.

"We... crossed paths. A few years ago. A mutual acquaintance introduced us at a gallery. He had a very fixed idea of how ladies should behave." Her lips pressed into a line. "We didn't get on."

"You were one of the first back in the drawing room when his body was discovered," Ginger said. "You seemed calm."

Miss Plimpton blinked. "Did I? I felt numb. I always feel numb when there's shouting, or..." She faltered. "When things turn violent."

"Were you in this room the entire time?" Basil asked.

"No," she squeaked out. "I slipped out to the powder room. Just for a moment. I—I needed a breath."

"Did you see anyone else?" Ginger asked.

Miss Plimpton shook her head. "I passed no one. I heard voices, footsteps maybe, but I didn't see anyone."

There was a pause. The fire popped softly in the hearth.

"Forgive me," Ginger said, her tone almost tender, "but you don't quite fit with this group. The others have long histories. You're a bit of an outlier."

Miss Plimpton's chin lifted a fraction. "Yes. I know."

"How did you get invited?" Basil asked.

Miss Plimpton's voice dropped. "He owed me. My paintings—Lucien said they would be shown. He promised. I thought he invited me to make himself feel… magnanimous."

"Were you nervous about them being displayed?" Ginger asked.

"I was terrified." Miss Plimpton's hands gripped her teacup again. "But I wanted them seen. I wanted people to understand. Of course, then it all turned out so—differently." She put down the teacup with a rattle on its saucer.

There was another silence. Outside, wind dragged its fingers down the side of the house.

"Well," Ginger started, "thank you, Miss Plimpton. That will be all for now."

Miss Plimpton stood quickly, nearly knocking her saucer. She steadied it, then looked at them both.

"I know I don't belong here," she said. "Not really. But I was invited, and I had a right to be seen. Just once."

She turned, hesitated, then added over her shoulder, "Most people don't really see me. But you did. Thank you for that."

She slipped away, her figure quickly swallowed by the gloom at the edge of the room.

Ginger and Basil sat in silence for a moment, the echo of her words settling.

"She's the only one here with nothing to prove," Basil murmured.

"Or everything," Ginger replied.

They exchanged a look. No conclusions yet. But something about the high-pitched lady with the trembling hands and the manuscript wings wouldn't quite leave them.

CHAPTER TWENTY-ONE

*D*elphine Valentino reclined on a carved mahogany settee, a crystal glass of brandy cradled loosely in one hand. The firelight gilded the embroidery on her navy gown, picking out tiny seed pearls stitched into the sleeves. Her dark hair, slightly mussed now from the long evening, was pinned low at her neck with a single sapphire comb. Despite her air of studied poise, her expression was drawn, the corners of her mouth set in a line too rigid to be merely bored.

When Ginger and Basil approached, she did not feign surprise.

"Do be quick," she said, swirling the amber liquid. "I've only enough patience left for one scandal at a time."

"Miss Valentino," Ginger said gently, taking the vacant chair opposite, "you mentioned earlier that you weren't with Mr. Zane when you left the room."

Miss Valentino offered a wry smile. "Still chasing ghosts, are we? I told you—I stepped out alone. I needed a moment. One can only endure so many barbed silences and unspoken accusations before the walls start to press in."

"And where did you go?" Basil asked, voice even.

"Not far. The music room. I thought I might find a breath of quiet." She took a sip of her drink, then added with dry contempt, "I found a dust-choked pianoforte and a draught under the door instead."

"Did anyone see you?" Ginger asked.

Miss Valentino gave a nonchalant shrug. "Only shadows. Though I doubt they'll give sworn statements."

Ginger let the moment breathe before pivoting. "You've made no secret of your feelings about your brother."

Miss Valentino laughed softly—once, without humour. "Lucien was a ghastly man with a brilliant mind and no heart. You may quote me."

"You didn't like him?" Basil asked.

"I despised him," she replied, her tone measured but laced with something acidic. "He exploited

175

people. Their secrets, their missteps. I was no exception."

"And Dorian March?" Basil asked, watching her closely. "What was your relationship to him?"

Her mouth twitched, and for the first time, her composure cracked. "Dorian was... complicated."

"In what way?" Ginger asked.

"We were lovers once. Briefly." She stared into the fire. "He was clever, relentless, and utterly incapable of letting anything lie. If Lucien collected and buried secrets, Dorian dug them up, dusted them off, and held them to the light until they screamed."

"Who ended the affair?" Basil asked.

"I did," she said softly. "He never quite forgave me."

"Did he threaten you?" Ginger asked.

"No. But he watched. Always watched. He said he was saving me for the right story."

Ginger exchanged a glance with Basil. "Did you feel threatened by him tonight?"

Miss Valentino didn't answer right away. "Not threatened," she said finally. "Exposed."

"We understand Lucian and Dorian weren't, er, well-liked," Basil started. Miss Valentino scoffed as Basil continued, "But is there anyone you suspect of their murders?"

"Have you talked to his sneaky assistant?" Miss Valentino asked with a smirk. "Talk about a snoop. I caught him in my room once, looking through my things."

"Hardly makes him guilty of murder," Basil returned.

"Endicott's been pilfering from Lucien's collection," Miss Valentino said with a flick of her wrist. "Minor works. Preliminary sketches. Things Lucien either wouldn't miss or couldn't remember owning. Endicott sold them through obscure dealers, under assumed names. Nothing large enough to make headlines—but enough to profit."

"Did Lucien know?" Basil asked.

"No. Not as far as I'm aware. But Dorian did. And he was planning to expose him."

"In print?" Ginger asked.

"Of course. He'd already begun writing. He said it would be a 'exhibit of duplicity.'" Miss Valentino shook her head. "He couldn't resist the flourish."

"Did Endicott know March was preparing an exposé?" Basil asked.

"Hard to say," Miss Valentino replied. "But Dorian wasn't exactly discreet. He called Endicott a crook to his face on Monday. Loudly. In front of several guests at the gallery."

"And you?" Basil asked. "Where do you fit between Lucien and Dorian?"

She looked up at him then, the firelight catching the shimmer of tears she refused to shed. "I survived them."

Her words hung in the air—part curse, part confession.

"Did you see Mr. March before he died?" Ginger asked gently.

"I passed him in the corridor. Briefly. He looked smug, as usual. I didn't stop."

"And after that?" Basil asked.

"I returned to the drawing room. The others were already whispering by then. I knew something had happened. But I didn't ask."

Ginger stood. "Thank you, Miss Valentino."

Miss Valentino drained the last of her brandy in one smooth motion and turned her gaze back to the fire.

Endicott sat ramrod straight on the edge of an embroidered chaise, his hands clasped over his knees as if bracing for impact. His spectacles had slipped slightly down the bridge of his nose, and a fine sheen of sweat glistened beneath the soft fringe of his light hair. His pinstripe waistcoat was impeccably buttoned, but the starch in his collar had begun to wilt.

He had the look of a man who had spent the last half hour trying very hard not to look suspicious—and failing.

Ginger and Basil approached him where he sat, alone near the sideboard. Ginger's heels made a soft tap against the parquet floor as she crossed to him.

"Mr. Endicott," she said with gentle formality, "may we have another word?"

His head jerked upward. "O-of course." He cleared his throat, then stood, bobbing in a half-bow before sitting back down at Ginger's gesture.

Basil remained standing, arms folded, a shadow against the mantel.

Ginger took the chair opposite. "Please tell us again, how would you describe your relationship with Mr. Valentino?"

Endicott opened his mouth, then closed it again. "Complicated," he said finally. "He was brilliant. And impossible. He could elevate a p-pencil sketch to gallery status with a word—and ruin a reputation in the same b-breath."

"Did you admire him?" Ginger asked.

"I admired what he could do with a c-canvas," Endicott said. "Less so what he did with people."

"Miss Valentino has suggested that Lucien

exploited the people around him," Basil said. "Would you agree?"

Endicott hesitated. "I think Mr. Valentino believed that the truth—his version of it—was always worth exposing. He had no concept of p- privacy. Or restraint."

"And Dorian March?" Basil asked. "How well did you know him?"

Endicott looked uneasy. "I wouldn't say I knew him w-well. He came around the studio occasionally. As I've mentioned before, he and Mr. Valentino had a long and... unsettled h-history."

"Unsettled how?" Ginger prompted.

"They'd been close once. Mr. Valentino helped l- launch his early writing career, then cut him off completely. After that, March turned his p-pen on Mr. Valentino and never stopped."

"You didn't like him," Basil said.

"I didn't trust him," Endicott corrected. "He was always circling, looking for s-something to expose."

"Something like theft?" Ginger asked evenly.

Endicott froze. "I beg your p-pardon?"

"Minor works," Basil said. "Sketches from the studio. Sold under assumed names through third- party dealers."

"I—" Endicott blinked. "Where are you g-getting this?"

"It's come to our attention that March discovered what you were doing," Basil said. "That he planned to publish it."

Endicott's face went a mottled shade of greyish pink. "That's—preposterous. I—anything I h-handled was approved. I catalogued what Mr. Valentino gave me."

"But you didn't always return what he didn't use?" Ginger offered.

"It wasn't theft," Bernard snapped, then immediately winced. "I mean—Mr. Valentino didn't m-miss them. Half the time, he left p-pieces lying about, discarded, unfinished."

"But you profited," Ginger said.

Endicott swallowed. "Not much. A few p-pounds here and there. Enough to pay off debts. I never touched the major works. And I n-never used his name."

"March called you a 'crook,' didn't he?" Basil asked. "To your face."

Endicott's jaw tightened. "Yes. In f-front of half the staff at the Holland Park Gallery. He enjoyed humiliating p-people."

"So when he threatened to publish what he knew?"

"He never said it outright. Just… hinted. Like he always did. S-smug little smiles. And questions that weren't really questions." His voice cracked. "I asked him to s-stop."

"But he didn't," Ginger said.

Endicott looked down at his hands. "No."

"Did Lucien know?" Basil asked.

"I don't know," Endicott whispered. "If he did, he n-never said anything. P-perhaps he wanted March to dangle it over me. Or perhaps he just stopped c-caring."

"And where were you when Mr. March was killed?" Ginger asked.

Endicott blinked at her, then looked helplessly around the room. "I—I was getting a drink. I thought he'd gone upstairs. I didn't see or hear anything."

Ginger watched him for a long moment. "Is there anything else you'd like to tell us, Mr. Endicott?"

Endicott shook his head, slowly. "Only that I didn't k-kill either of them. I may have made some … p-poor decisions, but not that one."

His voice trembled, and he looked genuinely frightened now—not only of being accused, but perhaps of whoever was still at large among them.

"Perhaps, you should give Zane a c-closer look, when he dares to show his face again."

"And why is that?" Ginger asked.

"He's a posh scoundrel."

Ginger noted that Endicott's tongue had no problems with those slanderous words.

CHAPTER TWENTY-TWO

$\mathcal{T}$he air was tinged with smoke and tension, and the fire in the grate crackled as it sank deeper into embers. Shadows reached long fingers across the polished floor as the storm outside rattled the tall windows.

Ginger stood near the hearth, her arms folded beneath the folds of her silk evening wrap. Her champagne gown shimmered slightly as she shifted her weight, eyes trained on the doorway. Basil, leaning beside the marble mantel, had one hand in his pocket and the other resting lightly on the edge, his gaze scanning the room for the hundredth time.

Felicia stepped inside, framed for a moment by the candlelight behind her. Her silver lamé gown was damp at the hem, and her carefully waved brunette hair clung in soft curls to her temples. Her breath misted faintly in the chill air as she entered.

She moved across the room quickly, weaving past Lady Horatia's disapproving stare and Lady Partridge's narrowed eyes, until she reached Ginger and Basil near the hearth.

"Mr. Zane is not in the gallery," she whispered, voice tight with concern. "Nor the music room, the library or the east corridor. We even checked the side parlour and the old smoking room. Nothing."

Ginger straightened. "And upstairs?"

Felicia nodded, catching her breath. "We tried the guest rooms—though most aren't properly in use— and even poked our heads into the linen closet."

"No sign of him at all?" Basil asked, his voice pitched low.

"None." Felicia glanced over her shoulder. "And I asked the footmen discreetly—he didn't see anyone leave the drawing room, not since the storm began. The front and rear doors are still bolted. Charles is searching the back hall and staircases. He said he wouldn't stop until he's looked in every cupboard."

Ginger's expression darkened as she stepped closer to the window, where condensation fogged the glass. Outside, the rain had turned to icy sleet, hammering the panes and glinting on the terrace stones where the light from the room fell through the window.

She turned, her gaze sweeping the faces around the room. Lady Partridge was sipping tea with the serenity of someone who'd already cast her vote. Lady Horatia appeared to be making a deliberate effort not to look at anyone at all. Several guests sat slumped in various degrees of unease, jackets rumpled, gloves discarded, their fine evening wear now wrinkled and dim in the firelight.

"I think," Ginger said softly, "we're past coincidence. First Mr. Valentino, then Mr. March; and now Nathaniel Zane vanishes. And just as questions begin to close in. Delphine Valentino said she wasn't with him."

"Which may be true," Basil muttered. "Or may be convenient."

Ginger looked toward the far corner of the drawing room. Vivienne Brousseau sat apart from the others, her pearl gown gleaming dully in the firelight. A dark shawl had been pulled tight around her shoulders, her gloved fingers clenched together in her lap. She stared into the flames as if searching for a signal only she could read.

Basil moved across the room and paced slowly near the drinks trolley, fingers drumming silently against the glass decanter. He'd removed his jacket earlier, and now his shirtsleeves were slightly rolled —more detective than dinner guest. From time to time he shot a look toward the windows, likely trying to gauge if or when the storm would abate and the roads become passable.

Guests dozed or drifted into silence. Lady Partridge's chin had sunk onto her chest, her lips slightly parted in the unflattering honesty of sleep. Endicott sat stiffly upright, but his eyelids drooped perilously, and he started with every creak of the floorboards. Vivienne Brousseau had now folded her arms tightly and closed her eyes, murmuring softly in French under her breath, as though praying—or cursing.

Delphine Valentino sat bolt upright, but her breathing was slow, rhythmic. A single glove dangled from one hand, forgotten. Even Lady Horatia, perched rigidly on a chaise, had gone uncharacteristically still, her gaze unfocused, lips pressed into a line of private dread.

Ginger stifled a yawn and paced to the window. Her head throbbed faintly behind her eyes, her limbs heavy as lead. Every muscle longed for rest, but her thoughts wouldn't let her stop. She sipped cooling tea from a China cup Betty had pressed into her hand earlier. The liquid barely stirred her senses.

Then—footsteps. Fast. Booted.

The drawing room door swung open and Alfred stood in the frame, breathing hard from the walk back from the service corridor, his hair standing on end and his cheeks flushed.

"Madam—sir—" he panted. "The telephone line's come back. We've got signal down in the housekeeper's room."

Ginger straightened, the room snapping to attention around her. Basil was already moving, shrugging into his jacket.

"Good," he said. "I'll put a call through to the local authorities—"

But he didn't finish.

A second sound broke through—the thudding of heavier steps, the cry of someone rushing—and then the door burst open again.

Charles stood in the entrance, pale and breathless, his cravat askew and dust clinging to the hem of his trousers.

Ginger's heart sank.

"I found him," Charles announced, his voice hoarse and ragged. "Zane."

"Where?" Basil demanded, crossing the floor in a flash.

"A storage room behind the west gallery," Charles said. "It's used for props and costumes for amateur theatricals. It was locked—from the outside. With a brass hook."

Basil froze. "Locked?"

"I forced it open," Charles said. "He was inside. On the floor."

Ginger stepped forward. "Is he—?"

Charles met her eyes, and there was no ambiguity there. "Dead. No question."

A collective gasp rippled through the room. Delphine Valentino let out a strangled cry and reached for the arm of a chair to steady herself.

Felicia turned away and covered her eyes. Endicott mumbled something under his breath.

Vivienne Brousseau rose slowly to her feet, as though the words had physically unseated her.

Lady Horatia swore under her breath—uncharacteristically unladylike.

Ginger looked around the room, now more than ever seeing not tired guests—but a house of suspects.

"That's three deaths," she said flatly. "In one night. Under this roof."

Lady Partridge shivered. "First the snake, then the spider, now the fly."

Miss Valentino whispered, "But why Nathaniel? He wasn't... important."

"He may have known something," Ginger said. "Seen something. Something worth killing for."

Felicia's voice trembled. "The police—surely—"

"The footman has gone to ring them," Basil said. "Until they arrive, no one leaves this room."

Ginger moved to Basil's side and spoke in a lower voice. "We're running out of suspects."

"And out of time," he said. "The killer's not panicking anymore. They're finishing what they started."

Ginger drew in a breath. Exhaustion clawed at her spine, but she pushed it down. There would be time to rest when this nightmare ended.

"Then we'd best find out what Mr. Zane knew," she said. "Before someone else dies."

CHAPTER TWENTY-THREE

The door to the west gallery's side room hung ajar, the brass hook that had sealed it now dangling uselessly against the wood, swaying slightly with each breath of the drafty corridor. Ginger paused in the threshold, a shiver prickling her spine. The air beyond was soured—mildew and mothballs mingled with something far more sinister: the sweet, metallic tang of death.

Basil stepped through first, lantern raised, its beam cutting across the murk. The small storage room lay steeped in shadow, the walls lined with sagging shelves heavy with faded plumes, opera cloaks, powdered wigs, and cracked papier-mâché masks whose painted eyes glared blindly back.

Mr. Zane's body lay crumpled between a toppled

costume trunk and an overturned chair. His head was twisted at an odd angle, his arm pinned beneath him as if he'd tried to catch himself too late. His suit, rumpled and dusty, was streaked with something darker, like soot or smeared rouge from a fallen theatre mask. His tie dangled loose around his neck, the knot skewed, as if he'd clawed at it.

Ginger stepped in after Basil, the floorboards creaking beneath her. Her gaze swept the corners. "No blood," she said softly.

Basil crouched beside the body, brushing a curl of hair from the nape of Zane's neck. "There's a contusion here—at the base of the skull. Could've been slammed against the trunk's edge. Or—" he tilted the head slightly "—a forceful twist. Snapped neck." He turned to Charles who'd stepped into the room after them. "Please ensure everyone is rounded up in the drawing room. No one is to be left unaccounted for."

"I'll take care of it," Charles said soberly.

"No signs of a struggle," Ginger murmured, scanning the nearby shelves. "No mannequins knocked over. No trailing fabric. Mr. Zane was caught off guard." She turned back to the costume trunk. It had spilled open during the fall, disgorging its theatrical contents in a chaotic fan: cloaks of faded velvet, an old military tunic with dulled buttons, a half-masked Arlecchino costume with a missing ruff. She crouched, pushing aside a plume-trimmed tricorne and a tangle of gauze.

Beneath the clutter, tucked beneath a ruffled shirt and a feathered hat, was a slim sheaf of programmes from family theatricals in the distant past—creased, ink-smudged, and oddly damp at one corner.

She drew them out carefully. The top one bore the familiar red-and-black insignia of the Zouch-Netherby family, but the sheet had been replaced upside down. The curling Z and N gave her pause. Something about it looked familiar. Familiar in a way she hadn't registered before.

Her gaze landed on a costume staff out of its place on the floor. She picked it up finding it to be surprisingly heavy. "If Mr. Zane came here willingly, the killer may have used this to hit him on the head." Her gaze fell once more on the body. "Then broke the poor chap's neck."

She moved to Basil's side. "Do you think he figured out who the killer was? Is that why he became the next victim? Or was he targeted from the beginning?"

"I wish we knew," Basil answered.

A gust of cold air blew in from the corridor behind them, and with it came the distant clang of the kitchen bell—startling, shrill, a reminder that the house was still pulsing with life, still full of footsteps and shifting shadows.

When they returned to the drawing room, everyone who remained at the manor had been gathered—guests and staff alike. The curtains were drawn against the night, and the fire, though stoked, cast little warmth against the chill of the small hours that had long settled over the room.

The drawing room had gone still again, but it was no longer the quiet of polite society. It was the quiet of dread. Of too many questions and not enough answers.

The staff had been summoned—Betty stood near the wall, wringing her apron. Alfred lingered just behind her, his young face pale, lips pressed tight. Mrs. Pell sat, rigid, near the end of the settee, her expression unreadable. Jones stood, statuesque next to the door.

Boss lay curled at Ginger's feet, head resting on his paws. His ears occasionally twitched at the sound of shifting limbs or the crackle of the fire, but he didn't move. Ginger found the weight of him near her ankles oddly grounding.

Basil remained standing, one hand on the back of a chair, his other resting lightly on a folded paper— Zane's catalogue, marked in pencil. His voice, when it came, was even, clipped.

"I hate to announce that Nathaniel Zane has been found dead."

Nola Plimpton suppressed a sob, her hand going to her mouth. Endicott shifted in his seat, knuckles whitening around the armrest. Lady Horatia closed her eyes. Her lips parted slightly, but no sound came.

"This is the third death in this house in less than twelve hours," Basil continued. "Mr. Zane was found in the costume storage room. His death appears… deliberate."

Silence. The kind that prickled.

"Is it the same person doing this?" Lady Partridge asked.

"We don't yet know," Ginger said, scanning the room. "But the timing, the method, and the isolation suggest this wasn't an accident. He may have been silenced."

"Silenced?" Miss Valentino repeated. "You mean —he saw something?"

Ginger gave a slow nod. "It's possible. And perhaps he was trying to prove it."

"Which means," Basil said, eyes sweeping the

gathered guests, "someone here thought he was close to doing just that."

The silence thickened.

Ginger's eyes roved the room. Every face looked different now. Greyer. Tighter. Either shrinking from suspicion or trying to hide behind civility. Even Lady Horatia, always the calm in the storm, looked… rattled. A sheen of perspiration had broken along her brow. Her fingers flexed and curled again, as if she couldn't quite control them.

The guests began murmuring in low voices. No one made eye contact for long.

Ginger looked down at Boss. He had lifted his head, ears pricked, and gave a soft, uncertain whine.

She reached down and stroked the space between his ears. "Come on, Bossy," she murmured. "Time to work."

Basil caught her glance. "Shall we convene in the study?"

She nodded. They needed a chance to talk in private. The pieces of this puzzle needed to be worked out and quickly.

Charles and Felicia agreed to keep the drawing room secure, as Boss followed Ginger and Basil out of the room.

CHAPTER TWENTY-FOUR

*T*he fire in the study had been revived, its flames snapping cheerily in the grate, yet the room still felt cold—less from the winter air than from the exhaustion and uncertainty weighing on them both. Ginger sat, legs crossed, the steam from her teacup in her hands coiling upward. Basil stood at the hearth, one hand resting on the mantelpiece. He stared into the coals as if they might arrange themselves into an answer.

The desk had been transformed into a battlefield of clues: a tie clip glinting dully, the bloodied letter opener, the broken brass hook from the dressing room door, a small glass vial stopper, and Mr. Zane's marked auction catalogue, its pages splayed like a wounded bird. A corner of the rug curled under the table leg, as though the carpet itself wanted to keep its distance from what lay atop it.

Ginger exhaled slowly, tapping her fingernail against her knee. "The problem is, we've eliminated everyone—and no one."

Basil turned from the fire. "Because no single person fits all three murders."

She nodded. "Lucien was killed practically in front of a room full of people. Dorian was stabbed alone, here in the study. Nathanial was ambushed and locked in. The methods are different. The timings are different."

"But the stakes are the same," Basil said. "All three were holding secrets. Or threatening to expose them."

Ginger's eyes narrowed. "And the only common thread is that Lucien knew all those secrets."

Basil crossed to the desk, leaning over the chaotic array. "What if it's not one killer?"

She looked up sharply.

"What if two are collaborating?" he said.

Ginger considered it, tilting her head. "But which two? We've accounted for nearly everyone during at least one of the murders, and never the same two people missing at the same time."

"Except Zane," Basil murmured. "And possibly

Endicott—he was never firmly placed during March's or Zane's time of death. Nola Plimpton drifted in and out. Vivienne Brousseau was present but none wittnessed her every move. Lady Horatia left the gallery briefly before Lucien died..."

"Even Felicia and Charles weren't constantly watching," Ginger admitted, rubbing at her temples.

Boss, who had been sniffing industriously beneath the settee, gave a short sneeze and then a low, intent grunt.

"What have you got, darling?" Ginger asked, rising to her feet.

The Boston terrier backed up, snuffling, and pawed at the fringe of the hearth rug. Basil knelt beside him, nudging the thick edge aside with the toe of his boot.

There—half-caught in the weave—was a fine, silvery strand.

Ginger crouched and plucked it delicately between finger and thumb, holding it up to the light. It shimmered faintly: pale, gossamer, unmistakably thread—delicate and expensive.

"That's from a lace cuff," she said.

Basil's gaze sharpened. "You're thinking what I'm thinking?"

"Nola Plimpton," Ginger said. "She's wearing a

silver-embroidered gown, with a wide band along the sleeve. But as the evening went on she hid her arms under her shawl. And now this…" She eyed the thread. "A stray from an impulsive stab, perhaps. Caught as she fled."

Before Basil could reply, there was a knock at the door.

Felicia swept in, cheeks flushed, her dark hair losing its finger curls as the night went on. "They've arrived," she announced, breathless. "The police. And the doctor."

Basil tucked on his jacket sleeves. "Finally."

"They came by horse and trap up the north track," Felicia continued.

Ginger glanced at Basil, then down at Boss, who wagged his stubby tail in quiet pride. "Then it's time," she said. "Let's see who flinches when the truth comes knocking."

THE FRONT DOORS had barely been unbolted when a blast of winter air tore through the entry hall, scattering ash from the hearth and setting the candles flickering in their sconces. Ginger stepped forward in time to see three figures stamping the mud from their boots on the stone threshold, rain sheeting down behind them.

Jones admitted two damp-looking gentlemen from the storm-slick dawn. The first was broad and barrel-chested in a peaked cap and oilskin, his sandy moustache drooping with the weight of water. The second, slighter, wore a tweed coat and carried a medical bag, his pale face pinched from years of treating coughs and chilblains rather than corpses.

"Inspector Dobbins," the officer said, removing his cap with the gravity of a man for whom hats were a serious business. "And this here's Dr. Simms, our village physician."

"Mrs. Reed. Chief Inspector Reed," Jones intoned with his customary dignity. "From Scotland Yard."

Dobbins blinked at Basil, then cleared his throat. "Didn't know the Yard was involved. We'd have sent word before, if so."

Basil shook his hand. "You weren't to know. I was on the premises as a guest when events occurred."

Dr. Simms gave a short bow. "Sad business. If you'll take me to the deceased?"

Basil led them toward the shuttered room where the bodies had been placed. The air cooled as they went, carrying the damp tang of the inspector's oilskin and the faint medicinal odour of Simms's bag.

Inside, Dr. Simms crouched beside the first shrouded form and lifted the sheet with professional reluctance. "Nasty wound to the chest," he muttered.

Inspector Dobbins winced. "Good Lord…"

"He fell into one of his own sculptures," Ginger said.

"Poor chap," Dobbins murmured.

Simms moved to the second body. "This one—stabbed in the back, you say?"

"Would you like help to turn him over?" Basil asked.

"No need, no need," Simms said hastily. "I trust you know a stab wound when you see one."

He gestured to the third form. "And this?"

"Broken neck," Basil supplied.

Dobbins shifted uncomfortably. "We've not had a murder in the village in thirty years—and that was over a prize sow. Settled before I even joined the force."

Basil's tone remained mild. "And your thoughts here, Inspector?"

The man glanced from one covered body to the next. "Three killings, no clear pattern. We can be grateful the guest list is short, but still… it'll take some sorting."

"Indeed," Basil said. "I hope you're not offended, but I took the liberty of ringing the Yard."

"You did?" Dobbins's brows rose, then he let out a slow breath. "Well… better to have the experts in, in a matter like this."

The relief in his face was echoed, faintly, in Dr. Simms's. The physician set down his bag with a nod.

"Until they arrive," Basil said, "please secure the grounds. No one leaves."

Dobbins straightened, glad to have his orders. "Yes, sir." Tugging his cap into place, he clomped off toward the front steps, the doctor trailing behind.

When the door closed behind them, Ginger looked at Basil. "You knew they wouldn't be up to it."

He allowed the faintest smile. "Call it professional instinct."

"And the Yard?"

"If the weather holds… Until then—"

"—we make good use of the time," Ginger finished, glancing toward the rain-streaked windows.

CHAPTER TWENTY-FIVE

Ginger was dismayed to see that it was Superintendent Morris who led the way. She and the superintendent didn't exactly see eye to eye—he found her intrusive, and she considered him an overbearing bully—but they had come to an uneasy truce. His overcoat was soaked at the hem and the thick shoulders gleaming with rain. He looked older than when Ginger had last seen him —more lined about the eyes, perhaps from the burden of a city growing no quieter. His hat was clutched under one arm, his hair clinging damply to his scalp.

Behind him, Constable Braxton, cheeks ruddy and expression stolid, wearing the official blue uniform and helmet, dragged in two leather satchels

—one marked with the Yard's insignia, the other plainly medical. Trailing them both was Dr. Wood, spectacles fogged, expression pinched with fatigue. He muttered something inaudible under his breath as he doffed his gloves.

"Well," Morris said his voice thundering as if addressing a large crowd. "Charming as ever, Lady Gold. Though I wouldn't call it welcoming."

"It's the wind," Ginger replied, "And the bodies, I suppose."

Morris gave a dry snort. "So I've been told. Three, is it?" His eyes narrowed as his gaze moved from Ginger to Basil. "What have the two of you been doing?"

"Our best," Basil said. "The killer is sly."

"Brilliant," Morris muttered, handing off his gloves to the butler. "Crime never takes a holiday, does it, Braxton?"

"Nor this storm, it seems," Braxton replied flatly, wiping his nose on a handkerchief.

Dr. Wood gave a theatrical sigh and straightened his coat collar. "It's sleeting sideways out there. I nearly lost my footing climbing out of that blasted gig, saving your presence, Mrs. Reed."

"We're just grateful you arrived at all," Ginger said truthfully.

"The bodies are in the cold room off the kitchen, Dr. Wood," Basil said. "One impaled, one stabbed, and one likely bludgeoned."

"If you'll follow me, Doctor," Jones said, with a slight bow.

"Well, you're not lacking variety, Reed," Morris said, "are you?"

"No sir," Basil returned. "Three separate crime scenes as well."

"Lead us to them," Morris shouted. Ginger wondered if the man really didn't realize how loud he was. Morris sniffed. "Braxton—bag and note-book, if you please."

As Braxton fumbled for his pencil stub, Morris turned to Basil with a pointed glance. "You've kept everyone on the premises?"

Basil nodded. "All present and accounted for. Guests and staff alike. No one's left without permission. They are in the drawing room."

"And no confessions yet?" he asked dryly.

"Only the silent kind," Basil said. "But I suspect one or two are beginning to crack."

Boss padded in from the hallway and sniffed at the superintendent's boots, then sneezed dramatically. Morris frowned down at him.

"What is that mutt doing here?"

Ginger scooped Boss into her arms before he got the toe of a boot up his backside. She scowled at Morris. "Boss helped to uncover a clue. He deserves a little respect."

Morris laughed out loud, as if Ginger had just made a clever joke.

Just wait until she solved the case, she thought protectively. Then the… unpleasant man would have something to laugh about.

Boots echoed on the flagstone as Ginger and Basil led Superintendent Morris and Constable Braxton down the corridor towards the first crime scene.

"I'd have thought murderers might take a holiday," Superintendent Morris muttered, tugging his collar higher against the chill. "A pleasant weekend in the country, a bit of gin, a roaring fire. But no. Can't even enjoy New Year's Day without someone getting theatrical with a corpse."

"This was theatrical even by Lucien Valentino's standards," Basil said.

"First stop?" Constable Braxton asked, flipping open a pocket notebook with calm precision.

Ginger gestured ahead. "Here. The alcove just off the main corridor. It connects the drawing room to the gallery."

They paused before the archway. The dramatic sculpture loomed at the back of the alcove like a spiked monument to hubris.

Superintendent Morris squinted toward the base. "This where you found the first victim?"

Basil nodded. "Lucien Valentino, the artist. Impaled through the torso. Looked as if he was giving his creation a big New Year's Eve hug. Likely died instantly."

"Dear God," Constable Braxton murmured. "What kind of sculpture is that?"

"An art piece with sharp opinions," Ginger said, dryly.

Superintendent Morris stepped closer, peering into the gloom. "This happened during the unveiling?"

"No," Ginger said. "This one wasn't part of the exhibition, it was already unveiled. But after the paintings were unveiled and sold in the gallery, the electricity failed, and everyone went to the drawing room. When next we looked into the corridor, he was dead."

"Hmph." Superintendent Morris paced the edge of the alcove, rubbing his jaw. "So what do we have? Someone approached him during the blackout and gave a good shove?"

"It appears they rigged tripwire," Basil said, pointing to the lethal device. "It had all been set up earlier. We think the killer counted on the distraction."

"Who was unaccounted for at the time?"

Ginger hesitated. "Lady Horatia. The hostess. No one saw her until after we had enough candles lit to see by."

Superintendent Morris sniffed. "Convenient."

"Perhaps. But circumstantial," Ginger replied.

They moved on.

The study still smelled faintly of woodsmoke and iron—blood and ash. Basil pushed the door open and stepped aside to let the others in.

A dried smear marred the floorboards near the desk. The overstuffed armchair remained tipped where it had fallen, a soft indentation left in the rug. On the little table, the bloody letter opener lay among the other pieces of evidence, long, elegant, lethal.

Constable Braxton hung back, quietly scribbling. Morris stalked the room like a hunting dog catching scent.

"The March fellow, wasn't it?" he said. "Stabbed here?"

"Yes," Ginger said. "Single wound. No struggle. Likely fatal within moments."

"Now, see, this one's different." Morris tapped the arm of the chair. "This is personal. Up close. That's someone who hated him."

The final stop was the storage room behind the west gallery.

The air grew colder as they descended into the less-used wing. Frost edged the corners of the windows, and a musty stillness clung to the corridor. Ginger unlatched the door, its splintered wood still bearing evidence of where Charles had broken through the outer latch.

Inside, the lantern's glow revealed a landscape of disorder. Costumes lay draped over chairs and mannequins, a brocade cloak had slid halfway from its hanger, and the open trunk gaped like a cracked mouth, its contents tumbling in a careless heap.

"Mr. Zane was found here," Ginger said quietly, pointing toward the empty space beside the trunk. "Neck broken. No sign of a struggle. It was quick."

"Lured in," Basil added. "Possibly drugged. Then finished off before he could react."

Superintendent Morris scowled. "What was he even doing in here?"

"Following a lead," Ginger said. "He found notes

—wrote margin scribbles in the gallery catalogue. He suspected something. Or someone."

"Ah." Superintendent Morris's eyes gleamed. "The amateur detective got too close to the truth."

He turned. "There's your answer, then. Whoever killed him is the same who killed Valentino."

Ginger shook her head. "Not necessarily. Mr. Zane may have seen something after Mr. Valentino died. Or after Mr. March. He may have been silenced for what he knew—not what he did."

Superintendent Morris exhaled hard. "Lord, I hate the countryside."

Basil chuckled. "The mud. The murder. The endless tea."

"And the opinions," Superintendent Morris muttered with a narrow side-eye directed at Ginger.

Behind him, Constable Braxton cleared his throat politely. "Superintendent, should I begin gathering statements?"

"Yes," Superintendent Morris sighed. "Start with that fussy butler. No one leaves until I say so. Not even the dog."

As he and Braxton turned to go, Ginger stepped aside, letting them pass.

She looked at Basil, and said with voice low. "He's going to chase every wrong theory in the book."

"At least he has the book," Basil said with a smile.

At that moment, Boss trotted in behind them with a soft sneeze, tail wagging.

Ginger crouched to ruffle his ears. "Let's solve this before Superintendent Morris arrests you for withholding evidence."

Boss licked her hand once in solemn agreement.

CHAPTER TWENTY-SIX

*T*he cold room lay in the farthest corner of the basement, accessible only by a narrow stone passage that trailed behind the kitchen. Used to store game during the shooting season, the chamber now served a darker purpose—an impromptu mortuary.

The whitewashed walls glistened faintly with condensation, beads of moisture crawling like slow tears down uneven stone. An oil lamp was hung on a nail above three butcher's benches that had been repurposed into makeshift slabs.

Chunks of ice lay beneath the slabs, melting into a rusted trough, creating a ghostly fog that clung to the ankles.

The air was sharp and metallic—clean, but in that

overly scrubbed, antiseptic way. Camphor. Vinegar. A hint of old stone and rusting iron.

Dr. Wood stood in shirtsleeves rolled to his elbows, thin spectacles pushed high onto the bridge of his nose. His movements were brisk and clinical, the easy efficiency of a man accustomed to death. A string of gauze dangled from his waistcoat pocket.

The three bodies lay beneath crisp white sheets, still and anonymous in death—three pale humps under the lamp.

Superintendent Morris hunched near the corner, his coat pulled tight and his hat jammed low, as if he could keep the cold out by sheer force of will. "I don't suppose this could've been done in the parlour with a nice coal fire?" he grumbled.

Dr. Wood didn't glance up. "Not unless you're fond of the stench of decomposition."

Constable Braxton stood just inside the door, his pencil scratching steadily across a page of clean, folded notes. His eyes were wide, but his jaw remained firm.

Ginger hovered near the entrance, arms folded tight against her chest. Boss sat beside her—subdued, ears low, nose twitching uncertainly at the cold, pungent air. He let out a small whine and pressed closer to her skirts.

Basil stood shoulder-to-shoulder with her, quiet and still. "I suppose this is as close to a chapel of rest as we're likely to get," he murmured.

Dr. Wood peeled back the first sheet with quiet precision.

"Lucien Valentino. Male. Mid-forties. No signs of struggle. No hesitation wounds. Entry point—lower left thorax, impaled through the ribcage. Penetrated the heart. Judging by the force and clean path, death was likely instantaneous."

Superintendent Morris squinted at the shadowed wound beneath the light. "Cause of death?"

Dr. Wood glanced up. "He was run through by a bronze sculpture spike, Superintendent. I daresay that'll do it."

Superintendent Morris grunted. "Right-o."

The doctor replaced the sheet and moved to the next body. The second form was slighter. The sheet came down.

Dorian March looked almost boyish in death. His sharp tongue and sharper gaze had evaporated, leaving only slack features and a faint shadow of surprise across his face.

"Dorian March. Male. Late thirties. Single stab wound to the back. Narrow entry between the sixth and seventh ribs—angled downward. The blade

215

likely pierced the heart or the aorta. Again, no sign of resistance. Likely died within seconds."

"Right-handed attacker?" Basil asked.

"Most likely. Clean insertion. No hesitation."

Dr. Wood replaced the sheet slowly, the corner fluttering like a sigh.

He turned to the third and final form.

"Nathaniel Zane. Male. Late forties. Severe bruising at the base of the skull. Dislocation of the C2 and C3 vertebrae. Damage suggests a forceful twist of the head or neck—quick, deliberate, likely from behind. A skilled move or a desperate one."

He leaned in slightly. "Note the dilated pupils. Could indicate sedation. Or fear. Either way, no defensive wounds."

"So," Superintendent Morris muttered, wrapping his arms around himself again, "we've got one skewered like a roast goose, one stabbed like a pig, and one wrung out like a damp towel."

He looked to Basil. "Not exactly a tidy pattern, is it?"

"No, sir," he said. "Three different methods. Three separate locations. Three very different kinds of death."

Dr. Wood took a small bottle of antiseptic from his pocket, poured a little into his palm, then rubbed it between his fingers.. "You'll have my full report once I get them into a proper mortuary and do the autopsies. But I'll save you the bother of waiting—it won't show a common thread. No shared tool, no consistent force or angle. If you're looking for surgical symmetry, this isn't it."

Superintendent Morris grunted. "So the killer's erratic?"

"Or," Ginger said quietly, "there's more than one."

Dr. Wood packed up his bag and headed for the stairs. "I've no fondness for clever crimes," he muttered. "Too many ways to go wrong."

Superintendent Morris nodded towards the bodies. "Too late for that now."

As the footsteps of the doctor faded, Ginger turned back to the marble slabs. The light of the oil lamp flickered overhead. A drop of condensation traced its way down the stone behind Dorian March's head.

Basil spoke softly. "Three methods. Three motives. But only one house."

Ginger's arms tightened across her chest. "And one storm to cover it all."

They stood together in silence, the cold seeping into their bones as if the room itself didn't want them to leave. Boss gave a faint, uneasy growl.

The return to the drawing room was meant to be grim but orderly—a regrouping after the sterile chill of the cold room, a moment to warm hands by the fire and begin the slow, methodical sifting of alibis and inconsistencies.

But as Ginger reached for the double doors, the tension hit first—not as a sound, but as a pressure in the air.

Then came the noise: a thud, a grunt, the sharp crash of glass.

Ginger shoved the doors open.

Inside, chaos.

Charles had Bernard Endicott by the lapels, dragging him bodily away from the archway to the side hall. Endicott flailed like a man caught mid-fall—sweating, red-faced, his polished shoes skidding against the carpet.

"You utter fool," Charles snapped, his voice tight with controlled fury. "What did you think you were doing?"

"I—I was only s-stepping out for air!"

"With your suitcase?" Charles hissed. "And your coat tucked under your arm like a footman's bundle?"

Endicott wriggled, desperate. "You d-don't understand—"

The guests had erupted into a flurry of motion. Delphine Valentino had sprung from the settee, one hand pressed to her cheek. Lady Horatia stood near the fireplace, trembling faintly, lips parted in stunned silence. Vivienne Brousseau had half-risen, frozen mid-step. Nola Plimpton clung to the carved arm of her chair as though the floor might fall away.

Superintendent Morris strode in behind Ginger, his voice already raised. "What the devil is this?"

Charles gave Endicott one final shove. The man stumbled, catching himself on the wingback chair before collapsing into it with the grace of a marionette whose strings had been cut.

"I found him skulking through the back corridor," Charles said, smoothing his waistcoat with restrained violence. "Suitcase in hand. He was halfway to the servants' stair before I caught up."

"I wasn't r-running!" Endicott barked. "This house—this n-night—it's unbearable! I n-needed air!"

"With a packed case?" Basil said coldly, stepping past Ginger. "You expected a change in altitude?"

Superintendent Morris stepped forward, face like flint. "Mr. Endicott, consider yourself officially detained for questioning. Until further notice, you don't so much as reach for a handkerchief without my say-so."

Endicott's legs folded again, this time with no resistance. He sank into the chair, breath heaving, a bead of sweat tracing down his temple. His mouth opened and closed, but no defence came.

Constable Braxton slid neatly into position by the drawing room door. He jotted a note with crisp, fluid movements.

Charles adjusted his cuffs, still bristling. "I saw a shadow pass down the corridor from the upper landing. Odd, I thought. Then I noticed the glint of a handle. Thought I'd go investigate."

"You did well," Ginger said softly. "That may have spared us another disappearance."

"Or another corpse," Basil muttered under his breath.

Superintendent Morris turned on his heel and surveyed the room.

"No one else leaves," he said, his tone cold and unflinching. "Not for tea. Not for a cigarette. Not to look at the weather or weep in the corridor. Not unless I say so. Is that understood?"

"Even the lavatory, Superintendent?" Lady Partridge inquired, raising an arched brow.

Superintendent Morris shot her a glare. "Escort and a time limit."

She sniffed. "Efficient.."

Basil leaned toward Ginger. "That wasn't a whim or a panic."

"No," she said, eyes narrowed. "He wasn't running from something. He was trying to vanish before something caught up with him."

Across the rug, Boss let out a low growl, the kind reserved for cats in the garden or squirrels that got too bold. His ears pinned back, eyes fixed unblinkingly on Endicott.

CHAPTER TWENTY-SEVEN

Superintendent Morris loomed over Endicott. "Well then," he declared, hands planted on his hips, shoulders squared. "There's your man."

Endicott blinked, sweat pooling along his upper lip. "I—I don't understand—"

"Oh, don't you?" Superintendent Morris snapped. "Three murders. One desperate escape attempt. A panicked expression. I've seen it all before. And I'll wager half your fine neckties you've got blood on your hands—and not just metaphorically."

"I didn't kill—" Endicott stammered, voice cracking. "I'd never hurt Mr. Valentino."

"Save it for the magistrate." Superintendent Morris reached into his coat, pulling a pair of handcuffs with a rusty jingle. "You, uh, whatever your name is, I'm placing you under arrest for the murders of, uh, Lucien Valentino, Dorian March, and Nathaniel Zane."

"Superintendent," Ginger said calmly from beside the fireplace.

All eyes turned.

She stepped forward, poised and unflinching. "If I may have a moment?"

Superintendent Morris let out an impatient sigh. "Oh, what now, Lady Gold?"

Ginger opened a palm. Inside rested a polished gold tie clip, engraved with two graceful, curling initials: NZ.

"We believed this belonged to Nathaniel Zane," she said, "and that he dropped it during the act of murdering Mr. Valentino."

Ginger turned toward Lady Horatia, as she flipped the tie clip upside down. "It's not N.Z. though, is it? It's Z.N. for Zouch-Netherby."

A breath caught. The room seemed to contract.

The air cracked—like ice dropped into scotch.

Lady Horatia's cheeks flushed. "That's madness."

Ginger stepped closer, holding the tie clip aloft. "Are you saying this didn't belong to your late husband?"

Lady Horatia's eyes flicked left, then right. Her voice rose with a tremor. "So what if it did? That doesn't prove anything."

"It proves misdirection," Ginger said coolly. "You didn't drop it by accident. You planted it—deliberately. Hoping it would point suspicion to someone else."

Morris pivoted slowly towards Lady Horatia. "Lady, uh, whatever your name is, you are under arrest for the murders—"

"Murder," Ginger interrupted softly. "Singular."

Superintendent Morris cleared his throat. "—of Mr. Lucien Valentino."

Lady Horatia sat stiff-backed in her chair, hands folded in her lap. Her silver-touched auburn bob had not a hair out of place, her expression was fixed and composed. But her gaze met Ginger's—not defiant, not ashamed. Simply… resolute.

"Very well," she said at last. "I did it. I killed Lucien Valentino."

A silence fell, thick and total.

She exhaled slowly. "I have lived with the shadow of my husband's death for nearly a decade. He was a patriot—a quiet hero. And yet no one beyond the corridors of Whitehall will ever know his name."

Her fingers clenched subtly in her lap. "Lucien

Valentino trafficked in secrets. In humiliation. He exposed people's private sins and whispered others just for sport. Somewhere in all that theatre, he hinted—without ever quite saying—that my husband had been compromised. That he'd betrayed his country."

She looked down. "I couldn't allow that to become his legacy. So yes—I planned it. I hosted the weekend. I pushed having Lucien's statue exhibited, even though it was not part of his preposterous auction. And when the lights went off for the second time... I guided Lucien's step."

She raised her eyes again. "It didn't take much. I didn't shove. I simply... turned him. And let gravity do the rest."

Superintendent Morris rubbed his face. "So who killed March and Zane, then?"

Ginger lifted her other hand, revealing a fine silver thread, looped around one finger.

"This," she said, "was recovered from the study where Dorian March was found stabbed. A thread from a very specific lace cuff from a specific evening gown."

Her eyes fell on Nola Plimpton. "Miss Plimpton. You've been hiding your right sleeve for most of the night."

Nola's eyes widened. Her lips parted in protest, but no words emerged. A strangled sob escaped her throat. Her composure broke.

She collapsed inward, shoulders heaving, tears streaking her cheeks. "Oh, dear Lord…"

She drew her arms into her lap, curling over herself.

"I didn't mean to kill him," she choked. "I loved him."

She looked up, eyes red-rimmed and glistening. "We had an understanding, a year or two ago. But Dorian changed. He became cruel. He held things over me—threats about forged recommendations, old debts. He said he could ruin me. That no one would care."

Her voice faltered. "When I saw him slip into the study, I followed. I thought if I could just speak plainly—remind him of what we had—"

Her lip trembled. "He laughed. Called me pathetic. He said I'd always be a little fraud in borrowed silk."

She pressed trembling fingers to her mouth. "The letter opener was just there. I didn't plan to use it. I didn't even think—I just… reacted."

Ginger stepped gently closer. "And once Lucien

was dead, you hoped whoever was caught for his murder would be blamed for Dorian's too."

Nola gave a tearful nod. "It was cowardly. I know that now."

Superintendent Morris sighed, long and loud. "That's quite a lot to pin on someone else's corpse." He turned and gestured at Endicott. "And this fellow here? What's his crime—besides cowardice?"

Ginger's voice was quiet. "He killed Nathaniel Zane."

Endicott sat unmoving, face pale, lips pressed in a thin line.

"You thought Mr. Zane was the killer, didn't you?" Ginger said. "You saw him snooping. Witnessed him taking notes. Whispering to guests."

Endicott gave a hollow laugh—dry and sharp. "Yes. I thought it was him."He leaned forward, elbows on knees, staring at the carpet. "After Lucien died, and then Dorian… I knew it wasn't coincidence. And Zane—he was everywhere. Watching. Asking questions."

"After the chief inspector and I questioned you," Ginger said, "you didn't return to the drawing room, did you?"

Endicott looked up with steely eyes. "I r-ran into

Zane in the corridor. I came up with a p-plan on the spot and told him I wanted to share something from Lucien's private papers. He followed me. I stunned him with a b-blow to the head. And then I... twisted."

"Because you thought he'd killed Lucien?" Basil asked.

"Because I thought it would end things," Endicott snapped. "If I eliminated him—then perhaps the killing would stop. P-perhaps I could change the story. Protect what little I had left." He exhaled. "But I was w-wrong."

The fire hissed softly. The clock on the mantel ticked once.

Superintendent Morris looked from face to face, then closed his notebook with a snap.

"Well," he muttered. "Motive. Means. Madness. That'll do." He groaned as he straightened. "Braxton —escort the lot of them out. We'll sort charges properly in the morning."

Constable Braxton nodded and moved toward the centre of the room.

Ginger turned back to the fire. The flames danced in the grate, warm against her face. Boss sat beside her, tail curled around his paws, eyes half-closed.

One a premediated crime; one a crime of passion; one a crime of convenience.

Three murders.

Three confessions.

Suddenly, there was a flicker, a hum in the wires, and with a soft pop, the crystal chandelier flooded the room with brightness. At the same moment, Ginger realised that outside, steadily and quietly, dawn had come, and a shaft of wintery daylight fell through the gap in the brocade curtains.

Finally—finally—the long night was over.

CHAPTER TWENTY-EIGHT

The sitting room at Hartigan House glowed with firelight and lamplight, casting a warm amber hush across time-softened Persian rugs and jewel-toned silk draperies. Rain tapped lightly against the tall sash windows, misting the panes and blurring the outlines of the garden beyond. A small brass coal scuttle gleamed softly near the hearth, where the fire gave a generous, steady heat.

A faint trace of lemon polish lingered in the air, mingling with the bergamot of Ambrosia's tea and the scent of ash from the burning logs.

Basil and Scout were hunched over the chessboard on a low games table. The lad, legs almost too long for his trousers, eyes sharper than ever, chewed his lip as he considered his next move. His thumb hovered above a knight, then shifted toward a bishop, then stopped.

"I know what you're doing," Basil said, not looking up. "You want me to take your pawn so you can fork me with the knight."

Scout grinned without denying it. "Would I really do that?"

Basil raised an eyebrow. "You'd do it without batting an eyelid."

On the armchair nearest the hearth, Ginger reclined with her baby daughter Rosa nestled beneath a quilt in her lap. Rosa gurgled softly, drowsy from milk and warmth, one tiny hand clutching the velvet ear of a well-loved rag doll. Her breath rose and fell in little sighs.

Ginger brushed a wisp of dark hair from Rosa's forehead and whispered, "That's Miss Penelope's ear, darling. Let's not pull it off." She gently disengaged the little girl's fingers from her toy.

On the settee opposite, Lady Ambrosia sat in a gown of navy wool with black velvet trim, her silver hair flawlessly coiffed, a diamond brooch winking at her throat. Her teacup was raised, halfway to her lips, as she surveyed the family scene with satisfaction.

"I must say," she announced, "I prefer January when it doesn't involve corpses."

"Seconded," Basil muttered, sliding a bishop into position.

Ambrosia continued, "I expected a scandal would come from the Valentino auction, but not three murders."

Boss snored softly in his tartan bed near the fire, ears pointed, one paw twitching in some dreamy pursuit of foxes or biscuits.

The wireless set atop the walnut cabinet crackled softly, filling the room with the cheerful syncopation of Henry Hall and the BBC Dance Orchestra. Brass and strings tumbled playfully over the hum of rain.

The music wrapped up with a rousing crescendo, and then the sound of Big Ben filled the room as the BBC news came on.

The announcer's clipped voice rang out with solemn clarity.

"—and now, a special bulletin regarding the events in the Chilterns on New Year's Eve."

Ginger looked up. Basil paused, mid-reach. Scout straightened on the stool.

"Scotland Yard confirms that all three individuals arrested in connection with the so-called 'Painted

Mask Murders' have been formally charged and remanded to separate facilities pending trial."

Boss lifted his head, ears twitching.

"Lady Horatia Zouch-Netherby, formerly connected with the Foreign Office, faces charges of murder in the death of renowned artist Lucien Valentino. Her legal counsel has declined to comment, citing national security concerns tied to her late husband's wartime service."

Ambrosia made a clipped sound and set down her cup with more force than necessary. "She'll be shielded, you'll see. Old ghosts and dusty secrets."

"Nola Plimpton, an aspiring painter, has confessed to the killing of her former lover, well-known writer Dorian March. Counsel for the Defense is expected to pursue a ruling of temporary insanity while under great emotional strain.

"Bernard Endicott, former assistant to Mr. Valentino, is to stand trial for the murder of Nathaniel Zane. The accused has no prior convictions."

The announcer cleared his throat.

"In a brief statement, Scotland Yard Superintendent Morris praised the investigative work of Chief Inspector Basil Reed, calling his efforts 'vital to the swift and thorough resolution of this troubling case.'"

Scout turned to look at Ginger. "He didn't mention you, Mum."

Ginger smiled faintly. "No, he didn't. No surprise there."

Basil frowned. "My men know the truth. Braxton was there. Word will get out across London." He walked over to kiss Ginger on the forehead. "Don't worry, love. Lady Gold Investigations will be busier than ever."

"And now, looking ahead to 1929," the announcer continued, "Parliament resumes on the ninth, the American stock market continues its erratic rise, and His Majesty King George V has expressed hope that the coming year brings stability across Europe and prosperity at home."

The music returned—a lilting arrangement of " West End Blues" that floated through the quiet.

Rosa shifted against Ginger's chest, her little fist curling around the hem of the doll's dress. She had fallen fast asleep, her breath warm and steady.

Scout tapped a pawn idly against the chessboard. "Do you think things will really be better this year?"

Basil glanced at Ginger. "If we keep our heads. And our hearts."

Ambrosia sniffed. "Let's not pretend. It's England. We'll muddle through, one scandal at a time."

Ginger smiled, pulling the quilt a little higher over Rosa's legs. "Whatever comes," she said softly, "we'll face it. Together."

And outside, beyond the rain-streaked glass, a pale shaft of afternoon sunlight broke through the clouds—soft as gauze, but unmistakably there.

A new year had begun.

If you enjoyed reading *Murder in the Painted Mask* please help others enjoy it too.

Recommend it: Help others find the book by recommending it to friends, readers' groups, discussion boards and by **suggesting it to your local library.**

Review it: Please tell other readers why you liked this book by reviewing it on Amazon or Goodreads.

* No spoilers please *

UP Next for Ginger Gold Mysteries

MURDER AT THE MAHARAJA'S COURT

Murder is a world away...

LADY GINGER GOLD never imagined her journey to Rajasthan would draw her into the glittering yet perilous world of a royal court. Invited with her husband Basil to a lavish celebration at a maharaja's palace, she is swept into a realm of jewelled elephants, opulent banquets, and the thrill of a tiger hunt in the desert.

But when a guest is gunned down during the hunt, whispers ripple through the gilded halls. Was the bullet meant for the victim—or for the maharaja himself? As Ginger unravels a web of intrigue, she uncovers dangerous undercurrents: British officials with secrets to hide, courtiers with shifting loyalties, and whispers of rebellion against the Crown.

Amid growing rebellion and corruption, Ginger must unmask a killer before palace intrigue turns deadly.

On AMAZON

ABOUT THE AUTHOR

Lee Strauss is a USA TODAY bestselling author of The Ginger Gold Mysteries series, The Higgins & Hawke Mystery series, The Rosa Reed Mystery series (cozy historical mysteries), A Nursery Rhyme Mystery series (mystery suspense), The Light & Love series (sweet romance), The Clockwise Collection (YA time travel romance), and young adult historical fiction with over a million books read. She has titles published in German and French, and a growing audio library.

When Lee's not writing or reading she likes to cycle, hike, and stare at the ocean. She loves to drink caffè lattes and red wines in exotic places, and eat dark chocolate anywhere.

For more info on books by Lee Strauss and her social media links, visit leestraussbooks.com. To make sure you don't miss the next new release, be sure to sign up for her readers' list!

Discuss the books, ask questions, share your opinions. Fun giveaways! Join the Lee Strauss Readers' Group on Facebook for more info.

Did you know you can follow your favourite authors on Bookbub? If you subscribe to Bookbub — (and if you don't, why don't you? - They'll send you daily emails alerting you to sales and new releases on just the kind of books you like to read!) — follow me to make sure you don't miss the next Ginger Gold Mystery!

Find me on Pinterest

www.leestraussbooks.com
leestraussbooks@gmail.com

MORE FROM LEE STRAUSS

On AMAZON

GINGER GOLD MYSTERY SERIES (cozy 1920s historical)

Cozy. Charming. Filled with Bright Young Things. This Jazz Age murder mystery will entertain and delight you with its 1920s flair and pizzazz!

Murder on the SS Rosa

Murder at Hartigan House

Murder at Bray Manor

Murder at Feathers & Flair

Murder at the Mortuary

Murder at Kensington Gardens

Murder at St. George's Church

The Wedding of Ginger & Basil

Murder Aboard the Flying Scotsman

Murder at the Boat Club

Murder on Eaton Square

Murder by Plum Pudding

Murder on Fleet Street

Murder at Brighton Beach

Murder in Hyde Park

Murder at the Royal Albert Hall

Murder in Belgravia

Murder on Mallowan Court

Murder at the Savoy

Murder at the Circus

Murder in France

Murder at Yuletide

Murder at Madame Tussauds

Murder at St. Paul's Cathedral

Murder at the Olympics

Murder at the Cave of Harmony

Murder in the Painted Mask

LADY GOLD INVESTIGATES (Ginger Gold companion short stories)

Volume 1

Volume 2

Volume 3

Volume 4

Volume 5

HIGGINS & HAWKE MYSTERY SERIES (cozy 1930s historical)

The 1930s meets Rizzoli & Isles in this friendship depression era cozy mystery series.

Death at the Tavern

Death on the Tower

Death on Hanover

Death by Dancing

Death on Tremont Row

Death at King's Chapel

THE ROSA REED MYSTERIES

(1950s cozy historical)

Murder at High Tide

Murder on the Boardwalk

Murder at the Bomb Shelter

Murder on Location

Murder and Rock 'n Roll

Murder at the Races

Murder at the Dude Ranch

Murder in London

Murder at the Fiesta

Murder at the Weddings

A NURSERY RHYME MYSTERY SERIES(mystery/sci fi)

Marlow finds himself teamed up with intelligent and savvy Sage Farrell, a girl so far out of his league he feels blinded in her presence - literally - damned glasses! Together they work to find the identity of @gingerbreadman. Can they stop the killer before he strikes again?

Gingerbread Man

Life Is but a Dream

Hickory Dickory Dock

Twinkle Little Star

LIGHT & LOVE (sweet romance)

Set in the dazzling charm of Europe, follow Katja, Gabriella, Eva, Anna and Belle as they find strength, hope and love.

Love Song

Your Love is Sweet

In Light of Us

Lying in Starlight

PLAYING WITH MATCHES (WW2 history/romance)

A sobering but hopeful journey about how one young German boy copes with the war and propaganda. Based on true events.

A Piece of Blue String (companion short story)

THE CLOCKWISE COLLECTION (YA time travel romance)

Casey Donovan has issues: hair, height and uncontrollable trips to the 19th century! And now this ~ she's accidentally taken Nate Mackenzie, the cutest boy in the school, back in time. Awkward.

Clockwise

Clockwiser

Like Clockwork

Counter Clockwise

Clockwork Crazy

Clocked (companion novella)

<u>Standalones</u>

Seaweed

Love, Tink

Printed in Dunstable, United Kingdom